The Christ

The Complete Trilogy

With Bonus Novelette

Jasper: A Siamese Story

by

Peter Scottsdale

Printed in the United States of America
First Printing, 2017
ISBN-13: 978-1975993658

ISBN-10: 1975993659

What People Are Saying About the Tales in
The Christmas Cat Tails

"The Christmas Cat"

"...heartwarming... great story to read if you have or have ever had a heart."
- Jessyca Garcia (Readers Favorite)

"Wonderful ebook"
- Crystal Martin (Amazon Reviewer)

"...beautifully touching..."
- Shar (Amazon Reviewer)

"...well written..."
- katyjane (Amazon Reviewer)

"The Christmas Cat 2"

"...definitely a story for all cat lovers...visual and alive."
- Mamta Madhavan (Readers' Favorite)

"Wonderful book...heartwarming and heartwrenching..."
- Kindle Customer (Amazon Reviewer)

"A nice inspirational story."
- trekker (Amazon Reviewer)

"The Christmas Cat 3"

"It's an enjoyable short read, that guarantees to stay with you for days after you've read the final word. Well done, Peter Scottsdale!"
- Joan Mettauer (Author of *Diamonds in an Arctic Sky*)

This book is a perfect example of why pets come into (and out of) our lives and help us heal ourselves.
- Linda Penner (Author of *A Hitman Is Cheaper Than Divorce: How to Stop Dragging That Breakup Ball and Chain*)

"Jasper: A Siamese Story"

"...very touching story..."
- Pat Meek (Author of *Goldie's Girls*)

Table of Contents

The Christmas Cat

He wasn't going to apologize. Fred had spoken his mind and be damned if he was going to apologize.

It was one day before the 25th, and they hadn't called. But again they hadn't called for the last two Christmases, either. So Fred sat, watching reruns of "Match Game" on the Game Show Network when he heard scratching.

It sounded like an animal at the door. He ignored it. Somebody's pet at the wrong door. Yet, it continued, annoying Fred as time and the scratching went on. A commercial came on and more scratching. Fred got up from his chair, deciding to scare the creature away. He left his basement suite and climbed the steps to the side door, his old knees hurting with every step.

He opened the door with a snap, hoping to scare the creature off. He opened his mouth to yell, but nothing there. The cold hit his face and ran down his unbuttoned shirt. Quickly, he closed the door. *Must be at least minus twenty out.* He hoped the scratcher had found someplace warm; nothing deserves to be out in such cold.

"Burr," Fred said and went back downstairs into his tiny suite, sitting in his worn chair. The game show was almost over, and Fred wondered if there would be Christmas themed game shows on that day. An old "Let's Make A Deal" with some of the audience dressed up as elves, reindeer, snowmen, Jack Frost, and Santa came on. *This'll do*, he thought.

Scratch, scratch, scratch. Fred heard it again. Not waiting for a commercial, he went upstairs and opened the door. The cold assaulted him so he barely noticed a small feline race inside and down the stairs into Fred's home. He closed the door and stepped back downstairs. He searched for the cat as he entered his kitchen then into the living room where he found the cat sitting beside the radiator, the warmest spot in his home.

The cat was a tortoiseshell with tabby markings. *A tortietabby*, Fred thought. Small paws and a shorter tail stood out to Fred. He wondered if she - he thought she was a girl, aren't all torties girls – had a place to live in this colder than normal winter. She meowed and Fred could hear a slight purr.

"Alright, get warm," he said and returned to his chair. He switched the channel to the Weather Channel and waited for the local forecast. Cold, dipping down to minus thirty degrees over night. Fred hated the cold and wished he could afford to live his senior years in Florida. But he was stuck here in the frigid north. He looked over at his new friend. She appeared gaunt, probably hadn't eaten in days. Fred got up and said, "Let's see if I have something for you to eat here. Maybe a can of tuna?" Her eyes were wide as she watched him go into the kitchen and search the cupboards.

"Nope, nothing," he said, and she meowed.

Fred pulled out his wallet and found thirty dollars he was saving to buy his grandsons Christmas gifts just in case he was invited over for Christmas dinner at his son's and daughter-in-law's place. But, they had not called. Again. And Fred was not going to call them.

With it being so cold, Fred didn't want to go out, but this cat needed a place to stay with food and a litter box. The grocery store was a ten-minute walk away, and it had what he needed for his new friend. So Fred got dressed best he could for the weather, took his wallet and ventured out into the cold.

Fred took care on the slippery sidewalks, as some lazy people hadn't cleaned off their walks. He walked – his foot slipping at little with each step – to the end of the block and turned left down busy Maple Avenue.

A young man approached him. When he got nearer, Fred nodded to him, and the young man said, "Merry Christmas." As the young man came breast-to-breast with Fred, Fred slipped on a patch ice. Falling down, Fred grabbed at the young man's hips. And down came the pants! This broke Fred's fall for he slid down to the icy sidewalk instead of landing hard and breaking a bone, or worse.

"Woah!" the young man said and immediately pulled up his pants.

"Sorry, sorry," Fred said.

The young man laughed and helped Fred to his feet. "Are you okay?" he asked Fred.

"Yes, I think so. Thank you."

"Well, have a wonderful holiday," the young man said and was on his way. Fred smiled. He liked that young man. The sun was shining this cold day.

Fred made it to the grocery store without falling again. He found the pet section and picked out a small bag of dry cat food, a litter box, and litter to go in it. He went to the cashier and paid $19.37 for everything. He put the cat food and litter into the litter box to carry it home. It was heavy, but he wasn't that old or out of shape that he couldn't carry it home. That was until he got outside. He knew he wouldn't get home carrying the heavy load.

He needed a ride. He thought of calling Sam, his son, however he doubted Sam would help. After all, it had been almost three years since they had spoke. *His wife saw to that.*

Fred hailed a taxi that had come into the parking lot. Grey-haired lady got out, and Fred got in. He knew it wouldn't cost too much for a two-minute ride home. He gave the cabbie his address and apologized for it being such a short ride.

"Don't worry about it," the taxi driver said. "We do short and long trips."

Soon, Fred was at his door. He paid the $5.25 fare and thanked him.

Going inside, He stomped the snow off his boots, hoping the noise wouldn't upset - who? - the cat needed a name. He found the small feline lying on his chair, curled up. Just looking down at that cat, he felt warm and secure. Fred had found a new friend, a new family member.

Fred took off his coat and boots and called, "Here, kitty." But she stayed on the chair until he poured out the cat food. The cat lifted her head with a snap and leapt to her feet. Instantly, she was at the bowl of cat food.

"What a hungry kitty," he said. "We need a name for you." Fred watched her eat. She purred as she ate, and he wondered how she did that. He smiled and thought of a name.

"Tahlia," he said. Somehow she reminded him of his wife before cancer took her spark for living and eventually her life. So he named her after his love.

Fred reached down, bending his stiff knees and let his fingers caress her mottled fur. The leather of her nose had different colors, black and orange with a speck of brown. Fred felt an affection for this cat that he hadn't felt since the last time he saw his grandsons. He missed it.

His knees hurt as he stood up to let Tahlia finish her meal. Fred left the kitchen returning to his chair and switching the channel on the t.v. "The Price Is Right" was almost on. But his thoughts drifted away from the television.

How are my grandsons doing? How they must have grown. I hope they call, but they won't.

During the first commercial break, Tahlia came and sat on the floor between Fred and the television and washed her face by licking her right paw and rubbing her face. *So cute,* Fred thought.

"Did you have a good lunch?" Fred asked her while she kept grooming herself. Soon Bob Barker was back on with another pricing game - the one with the yodeling mountain climber. Tahlia stopped grooming, stared at Fred, and soon jumped onto his lap. This made Fred start as he wasn't expecting it. He smiled and stroked her. She placed her front paws on his chest and pushed her face into his and purred. Fred laughed.

Soon, Tahlia was up on the back of the chair, and Fred could feel her sniffing his partially bald head. He only had hair around the sides of his head in typical horseshoe fashion with none on top. The hair he had was white and buzzed short. He liked it that way.

She started licking his hair, surprising him. Fred and his wife had had a Siamese she called Bubba that talked a lot but never licked his head. Even the cat his sister owned – a silver tabby – when they were kids never groomed him. Fred figured she needed to bathe him, and he liked it. It was affection for a lonely old man. Her rough tongue felt like a massage, but soon the licking started to hurt as Tahlia concentrated on one spot. He winced as she groomed. It was slightly painful, but he didn't want her to stop. So he moved his head to the left, and she focused on a new spot.

The Showcase Showdown was beginning when Fred realized no Christmas decorations were up. There hadn't been any hung since the last Christmas he had with his son three years before. But now he had company, a new addition to the household. Tahlia stopped licking him and jumped down. Fred got up and went to his storage room, pulling out his box of Christmas decorations.

He unpacked red and green and blue ornamental balls that go on the tree, tinsel, and garland. Then he remembered tinsel can seriously damage a cat's insides if eaten, so he packed away the tinsel and pulled out a small artificial tree. He stretched the collapsed tree from the top and bottom, and the branches popped out. A silver Christmas tree appeared. Next came the beautiful blue lights he loved.

Fred decorated the tree and soon found Tahlia playing with one of the red balls hanging from a low branch. He stood back from the tree, taking a good look. Something was missing. Presents. He gathered the gifts he bought his son and grandsons the last two Christmases that were never delivered. Already wrapped, the gifts were placed under the tree. *A fine looking tree,* he thought. *All that's missing is family.*

Fred sighed and remembered three Christmases ago to what he was now realizing was his mistake.

Sam and his wife, Jessie, had invited him over for Christmas dinner and gift exchange, and Fred was to spend the day. It started with the gift opening at 8am as soon as Fred arrived. They had waited for him. The youngest, Roger, was chosen to open his presents first. He was eight years old.

"Awh, why can't I go first? He always goes first," Joe – who was two years older – said.

"The youngest goes first," his mother said.

"Not fair," Joe said and crossed his arms.

Roger opened his gifts and soon after Joe followed. They each got toys, clothes, and a DVD movie. Then the adults were up.

From the youngest – Jessie – to the oldest – Fred. Fred opened a blue housecoat from the boys and a big screen t.v. from his son and daughter-in-law. Then the boys started to argue.

Joe wanted to watch his Teenage Mutant Ninja Turtles DVD first with Roger wanting his first.

"I want Sponge Bob," Roger protested, raising his voice.

Soon Fred's grandsons were screaming at each other, which got a response from their mother, who sent them to their rooms.

"If you can't get along on Christmas day, you can stay in your rooms," Jessie said.

The boys stomped upstairs to their rooms and slammed the doors. This angered Jessie, and she went upstairs, yelled at each of them, and confined them until dinner. Jessie returned to the living room.

"You shouldn't have grounded them to their rooms on Christmas day. It's Christmas, Jessie," Fred said. He had come over to see his family, including his grandsons.

"Fred, I've had enough of their fighting. If they can't behave peacefully, they can rot." Jessie's voice snapped.

"Rot?" Fred said. "You're a poor mother."

Jessie opened her mouth to speak but shut it without saying a word. She glared at Sam and pointed to the kitchen. Sam and Jessie stepped into kitchen, and Fred heard loud voices, mostly Jessie's. A few minutes later, Sam emerged and told Fred he would drive him home. Fred was angered and disappointed but got his coat and boots on, and they left with his gifts.

On the way back to Fred's basement suite, Sam said, "You shouldn't have called her 'a poor mother'." And that's was the only thing said on the drive there. Sam helped Fred bring in his gifts and said, "Goodbye." They had not spoken since. Three years minus a day.

Fred thought about calling his son. "The Price Is Right" was over, and Tahlia jumped on him again, looking to get petted and share a purr. Fred petted her. He needed to call his daughter-in-law first. He picked up the phone and dialed. She answered.

"Jessie, it's Fred."

"Yes," she said.

"Jessie, I want to apologized. I'm sorry for calling you 'a poor mother'. You were right. Whether it was Christmas or not, the boys shouldn't be fighting like that. I'm sorry."

A silent pause.

"Okay, hold on a minute," she said.

A minute later, Sam spoke into the phone. "Dad, would you like to come over for Christmas dinner tomorrow? We'd love to have you."

"I sure will," Fred said through a smile. "And I've got a new addition to the family I have to tell you about. See you tomorrow."

"I'll pick you up in the morning at eight so we can open gifts together again."

"See you then," Fred said and hung up. "Yes, yes, yes!" He picked up Tahlia and kissed her face. She meowed. Fred hoped the gifts he bought for the previous Christmases were good enough, because he was broke. But he would make the best of it. "This is going to be quite a good Christmas, Tahlia." And he hugged his new cat.

The Christmas Cat 2

Chapter One

- 1 -

"What do you say we get Chelsey a cat for Christmas?" Ken asked his wife.

"Christmas is less than a week away."

"That's perfect. We can go to the SPCA, and she can pick one out. I miss having a cat."

"After Red died, you said you didn't want another cat only to watch him die. It just hurt too much," Darla said and put the carrots Ken sliced into the pot.

"I still miss Red. He was such a beautiful orange one." Ken thought for a moment. "I think it's time for a new cat. It's been three years."

"Is this cat for Chelsey or you?" Darla laughed.

"Well, Chelsey. Obviously. But I can still love him." Ken stirred the soup.

"She'll love having her own cat...Okay, we'll go tomorrow afternoon. But I want to surprise her if we can," Darla said.

"I know how we can have her pick out a cat and surprise her Christmas Eve. It'll have to be Christmas Eve. It's hard to hide a new cat that'll probably meow all night in a new home. What do you think?"

Darla nodded and called her daughter.

Chelsey ran from her bedroom, down the stairs, and into the kitchen. "What? Is supper ready?" Her red hair dangled over ears and shoulders, and Darla loved her daughter's freckled face.

"Do you want to go to the SPCA Monday and get a new cat?" Darla asked her nine year old.

"Really?" Chelsey's eyes grew wide and sparkled. She clapped her hands together. "Really? For sure?"

"Well, we'll see what they have," Darla said.

"Oh, can I get a Tuxedo Cat? Please, please, please. They're so cute, and they look like they have a tuxedo suit on. Please," Chelsey said, drawing out the last "please" into one long word.

They both looked at their child and smiled.

"If they have a Tuxedo Cat," Ken said.

"They might have one," Darla said. "With your dad working evenings, we'll be able to go tomorrow afternoon."

"Aww, can we go now?"

"They're not open Sundays. We'll go tomorrow. Can you wait that long?" Ken said.

"If I have to." Chelsey pouted.

"Okay, we'll go tomorrow. So don't go anywhere tomorrow if you want a cat."

"Can Sue come over tomorrow then?"

"Okay."

"I'll go call her," Chelsey said and left the kitchen. "I'm getting a cat. I'm getting a Tuxedo Cat."

Her parents laughed. Darla turned to her husband. "Now, how are we gonna surprise her?"

- 2 -

The next afternoon Chelsey and Sue were playing with her stuffies in Chelsey's bedroom and talking cats. Sue had a "regular old Tabby" named Stripes that she adored. She loved to pick up Stripes and cuddle with him and kiss him over and over.

"He loves to be loved," Sue said.

"I want my new cat to be like that. We had an orange cat named Red. He was my dad's, but I'm gonna have my very own cat. A Tuxedo Cat."

16

"What are you going to call him?"

"I don't know, yet."

"How about Mr. Tuxedo?"

"Nah. I want something...something...I don't know. Something about his color. He'll be black and white."

"How 'bout Zebra? They're black and white."

"He won't have stripes. Zebras have stripes. He'll look like he has a tuxedo suit on. I know 'Suits.' I'll name him Suits. And he'll be really, really cute."

"You know what my mom makes me do? Clean the cat box. It's so gross. Sometimes I don't do it. And it stinks, and my mom gets mad, and then I have to clean it more. But I love Stripes. He's so soft. He likes to play with a feather on a string. And it's got a stick on it too so you can move it around. He hits it with his paws and bites the feathers." Sue laughed and Chelsey joined her.

"What are you two laughing about?" Darla asked after opening Chelsey's bedroom door.

"Sue's cat."

"My cat."

"Well, it's time to go to the SPCA. Your dad's ready," Darla said.

"Can Sue come?"

"No, dear. We'll drive Sue home before we go."

"Awww," came out of Sue and Chelsey's mouths.

"Come on, girls. Time to go."

"I'm getting a new kitty."

- 3 -

After dropping Sue off at her home, Ken, Darla, and Chelsey Ashton drove across Langston Falls to the local SPCA. Chelsey never stopped talking about her new feline that she didn't have yet.

They arrived at the SPCA, and Ken parked their Toyota Camry. Chelsey jumped out of the car and ran to the SPCA entrance. In she went and up to the counter.

"We want a Tuxedo Cat," she said to the large woman behind the counter before the woman could ask the excited little girl, "May I help you?"

Ken and Darla entered the building in time to hear the woman tell Chelsey, "We have two Tuxedo Cats up for adoption. If you're the right person for them. Are you her parents?"

"Yes, we are," Darla said.

"Ok, I'm Andrea, and there's an application that needs to be filled out after you pick out your cat, or rather, after he picks you out."

Ken and Darla chuckled. "What's so funny," Chelsey asked.

"Can they pick out a cat –"

"A Tuxedo Cat," Chelsey said, and Darla shushed her.

"—while I fill out the forms?" Ken asked.

"Sure," Andrea said. "There are four rooms with cats in cages with one cat in each room allowed out their cage at a time. So go ahead and check out our kitties. Each cat has a note on their cage with their names and some info."

"Ok, thanks," said Darla. "Let's start here." Across from the counter, Darla opened the door to room one. Chelsey and Darla went inside and shut the door.

Ken turned to Andrea and said," If she picks out a cat – probably a Tuxedo –"

"I gathered that."

"Yea, when can we bring him home?"

"There is a 24 hour grace period from being approved for adoption and paying the adoption fee before you can pick up your new friend."

"Can we extend that grace period to Christmas Eve?"

"The cat's a gift?"

"Yea, we wanted her to pick one out and then surprise her Christmas Eve. So if we could leave him here until – what time do you close on the 24th?

"Five p.m."

"That'll work. Can I pick him up just before close on Christmas Eve?"

"I think we can do that, but there might be a fee to house him a few days."

"That's fine," Ken said and picked up the clipboard and form and filled it out.

In the first room of adoptable cats, Chelsey and her mother found a Tabby named Rex. A friendly fellow but not a Tuxedo Cat. Tanzy, a Tortie-Tabby with bright white fur across her face, neck and chest, was not so friendly as she opened her mouth in warning as if to bite if Darla petted her again. And an older white Persian had a note on her cage that said she was there too long. Darla knew what that meant but didn't want her daughter to know that that cat was going to be euthanized soon. They moved onto the next room.

There they found a Tuxedo Cat with a medium length coat among another Tabby and a Siamese, who was out of his cage.

"How about this one?" Chelsey asked her mother. "His name's Boots, but I'll call him 'Suits.'"

Boots was lying on a carpeted shelf in his cage. He looked out at the two humans looking in at him. He had white whiskers on a black and white face.

"He's so cute," Chelsey said and stuck her fingers into the cage. Boots sniffed her and rubbed his face against her fingers. Darla put the Siamese in his cage and took out Boots for Chelsey to hold. Chelsey held him, and Boots fit nicely into her arms. He purred. The card on the cage said he was four years old. Chelsey pulled him close.

"Can we get him, mom?"

"Maybe, let's see the other cats first."

"He's the one. I know it."

"Okay, put him back, and we'll go to the next room."

"But what if somebody takes him before we can?"

"It'll be okay, Sweetheart. There's nobody else looking at cats right now."

Chelsey put Boots back in his cage, and they left that room and went into the next where they found an aww-dorable Tuxie. He was out of his cage and playing with a toy mouse. Chelsey laughed and got down on her knees to watch him. Darla checked out his note.

It said his name is Capone, and he's nine months old, a fixed male and front paws declawed. Darla liked that he was declawed that meant less of a chance of her daughter getting scratched. It also meant he would have to be an indoor cat. Without his claws, he has no way to protect himself from dogs, other cats and wild animals.

Chelsey reached out and scratched Capone behind the ears and around the neck, and he pushed into her hand. Capone was mostly black. He had white whiskers like Boots, white paws with black toes, a white design on his chest and belly, a black face with white down his chin and neck and a milk moustache.

Chelsey stood up and asked her mom, "I can't decide. What do you think?" But before Darla could answer, Capone jumped into Chelsey's arms and rubbed her face with his. This surprised and delighted both mother and daughter.

"He's the one! He's the one! Can I get him? Please, please, please."

"Okay." Darla smiled. She liked Capone too.

- 5 -

Darla and Chelsey came out of the third cat room, grinning and joined Ken at the counter. He had finished filling out the paperwork.

"I take it you found a puss," Ken said, looking at their smiles.

"Capone! Capone!"

"Yea, he's one cute kitty," said the big woman behind the counter. "But you can't take him today."

"Aww," said Chelsey.

"Maybe in a few days – after Christmas," Ken said. "They have to approve our adoption request."

"But what if someone takes him?" Chelsey said with some panic in her voice.

"Don't worry," said Andrea, "we'll keep him for you if we approve the adoption."

"Okay," Chelsey said resigned she wasn't getting Capone that day.

"Alright, let's go," said Darla. The Ashton family turned and headed out the door. Ken turned around and gave two thumbs up to the big lady and mouthed, "Thank you." And he was gone.

Chapter Two

- 1 -

Ken arrived at the Langston Falls SPCA at about 4:30 p.m. Christmas Eve. They were closing in a half an hour to get home early for the holidays.

When Ken walked in, the same large lady behind the counter said, "Merry Christmas."

"Merry Christmas," Ken said, smiling. "I'm here to pick up Capone. Is he still here?"

"Yes, he is. Oh good, you brought a cat carrier."

Ken put Red's old beige carrier on the counter. "Chelsey's gonna be so excited."

"Are you ready for your new friend? A litter box and food?"

"We had a cat before so we still have his old litter box, and we bought some Meow Mix yesterday."

"Good, I'll go get him," Andrea said. Taking the cat carrier, she went into room three. She returned shortly with Capone in the carrier. He meowed. She put the carrier on the counter and checked Ken's paperwork. Everything was paid up and filled out. The adoption fees were cheaper because Capone was fixed before he came into the shelter.

"Okay, you can take him home. He's such a cute kitty."

"Chelsey keeps asking about him," Ken said and picked up the carrier while peaking inside. "Let's get you home, Capone." Ken smiled and said to Andrea, "Thank you and Merry Christmas."

And then Ken and Capone left the SPCA. Ken, a happy guy – Capone, a frightened kitty.

- 2 –

When Ken got to his car, he unlocked and opened the passenger door. He placed the carrier on the front passenger seat and arranged the seat belt around it so it wouldn't move and clicked the seat belt socket into place. He pulled on the belt and was satisfied it would keep Capone safe if he had to hit the brakes hard on the way home.

"There you go, pussycat. All belted in."

Capone started meowing. Ken closed the door and went around to the driver's side of the car, got in, and belted himself in. He put the key in the ignition and started the vehicle. After putting the car in gear, he drove away.

Christmas carols played on the radio. Ken liked the oldies station for the mix of classic hits and Christmas ones. Hall and Oates, one of Ken's favorites, came over the radio with their version of "Jingle Bell Rock."

"Alright, some good music for us, Capone." Ken stuck his finger between the bars of the carrier's gate, touching the new kitty's fur. And Capone meowed some more.

Ken drove across town and slowly into the downtown core where the city had erected Christmas lights and displays. The sun was down, and the street was busy with last minute shoppers. But Ken knew he had the best gift of all.

He looked out his windshield at all the Christmas lights and décor, allowing them to dazzle his eyes. Red and green and blue. Candy canes, wreaths, and a Santa's beard. Ken smiled.

"Look at all the lights, Capone." More meowing.

After getting a good look at the lights, Ken decided it was time to get home. He left downtown Langston Falls, driving under the railway bridge and taking a right at the Tim Horton's donut shop onto Maple Avenue past the Corona Tavern where he used to

DJ on Friday nights. Ken and Capone went over the overpass and found the police on the other side, lights flashing.

Three cop cars blocked off the left and right turn lanes, leaving one lane to drive through. Several cars were stopped in front of Ken. He pulled up and stopped behind a dirty white Chevy. He saw a "Check Stop" sign and was glad he didn't drink and drive anymore.

Before he met Darla, Ken partied as a young man. Drinking a lot and driving when he felt like it. He considered himself lucky he didn't cause any accidents or get caught being over the limit. One night, he didn't remember driving home. Those days were over, and he was glad.

The three vehicles ahead of him were allowed through, and Ken pulled up to a cop who signaled him to stop. Stopping, Ken rolled down his window and turned down the radio. The policeman walked up to him.

"Evening, sir," the cop said. "Langston Falls Check Stop. Have you had any alcohol tonight?"

"Nope," said Ken.

"Any alcohol in the vehicle?" The cop shined his flashlight into the car and took a look.

"Nope."

Capone had stopped meowing.

"Have a good night," the cop said and waved Ken through.

Ken slowly drove twenty feet to the next intersection and stopped at the red light. He turned to Capone. "How are you doing in there, kitty-cat?" It was dark, but Ken could see Capone's milk moustache. The light turned green. Ken took his foot off the brake and pressed the gas, pulling into the intersection.

A blue SUV came through the red light and struck the driver's side of Ken's Camry - t-boned it - crumpling the driver's door. The SUV's bumper shattered the driver's window and pushed inward. The airbags burst open but were not enough to stop that bumper from striking Ken's head. The left side of Ken's head was crushed inward two inches. Instant death.

The Camry drifted to the right and came to a stop against the curb. The driver of the SUV was saved by her seatbelt and airbag. Capone was thrown around inside the carrier. Because

Ken had belted him in, Capone was more frightened then before but unhurt.

The policemen dropped everything and ran toward the accident with one of them calling an ambulance. One ran to Ken's car, and another to the SUV.

At the SUV, the cop opened the driver's door and checked on the woman inside. She was leaning back in her seat. A deflated airbag hung down from the steering wheel. She was alone. He smelled alcohol. A heavy stench. The 22 year old woman bled from a gash on her head that would need stitches but otherwise was not hurt.

An ambulance arrived within a few minutes. The paramedics got out and assessed the scene. Ken Ashton was pronounced dead, and the drunk woman was taken to the hospital. The police found Ken's address on his driver's license and were not looking forward to what they had to do next.

Chapter Three

At four o'clock, Chelsey got home from visiting with Sue, and Darla suggested they start decorating the house for Christmas. Traditionally, the Ashton clan would decorate after supper Christmas Eve, but Darla knew when Capone got here, Chelsey wouldn't want to decorate anything. She would just play with Capone.

They went into the basement and brought up the big cardboard box of Christmas decorations and the fake tree they used every year. Mother and daughter opened the box and found what they left last year.

Inside were boxes of lights not put away properly, a wreath, and plastic holly, ornaments of green, red, gold, silver, and blue and one special ornament with Chelsey's birthdate of "September 14" on it. Those old decorations seemed new every Christmas.

The tree - old and beaten up – was put up first. It had been with Ken and Darla since their first Christmas together twelve years before. The two girls hung tinsel, lights, and ornaments on the branches.

"Don't put any decorations on the bottom branches," Darla said, knowing cats love to play with ornaments.

"Why not?" Chelsey asked and placed tinsel on the tree.

"It looks better up higher."

"Okay," Chelsey said and moved a lower glass ball to a middle branch.

The two Ashton girls finished decorating the tree and hung up star decorations from the ceiling. They were done in about an hour, and Darla started wondering where her husband was. It was almost dinnertime. Maybe he had trouble with Capone. She hoped he got Capone or it would ruin the surprise. She decided to make supper.

Ken will be home soon, she thought.

Darla took the spaghetti sauce she made the night before out of the fridge and placed it on the stove. She turned the heat to medium and took out a large pot to boil the spaghetti. Supper was ready twenty minutes later and still Ken wasn't home. She didn't know if she should be angry or worried. *Where could he be?*

Darla came into the living room and found Chelsey watching "Rudolph the Red-Nosed Reindeer" on television.

"Supper time," Darla told her daughter.

"Goody. I'm hungry. Where's Dad?"

"He must be running late." Darla hoped she was right.

They ate the spaghetti – a family favorite. When Darla finished her dinner, she made a plate for Ken and put it in the fridge, and they washed and dried the dishes. Then they heard a knock on the front door.

– 2 –

Darla answered the door, and Chelsey stood behind her, looking around her to see who it was. Two uniformed police officers – a man and a woman - were at the door. When Darla saw them, she knew something was wrong. Chelsey didn't. Darla gasped.

"Mrs. Ashton?" one of them said.

"Yes." Tears welled up in her eyes.

"I am sorry to inform you that Ken Ashton was killed in a car accident this evening. I'm sorry for your loss," the policewoman said.

"Oh, God. Oh, God. Ken." The tears that had welled up were now running down her face.

26

"Daddy," Chelsey said and ran up to her bedroom, crying. Darla felt like throwing up and backed away from the door. The officers stepped inside.

"Mrs. Ashton, your cat survived the crash. He doesn't appear to be hurt," the tall cop said. He held out the cat carrier, but Darla just shook her head and burst out crying, wailing, and sobbing.

The policeman put the carrier on the carpet. Knowing there was nothing else they could do at that time, the officers again said they were sorry and left, closing the door behind them.

Darla's legs gave out, and she fell to the floor. "Why? Why? Why?" she kept screaming over and over. She stayed on the floor, mourning. Both her and her daughter cried themselves to sleep that night.

Chapter Four

- 1 -

The next morning – Christmas morning, Darla checked on Chelsey and found her still sleeping. So she went downstairs. Darla ignored Capone who meowed from the cat cage as she walked by and went into the kitchen. She telephoned her mother and, through tears, told her about Ken's death. Her mother, Grace, told her she was coming over. She arrived fifteen minutes later.

Grace knocked and opened the front door, finding Darla on the other side waiting for her mother. They hugged and cried, holding each other for a good long while until Capone started to meow.

Hoping to get her mind off Ken, Grace said, "Since when do you have a cat?"

Meanwhile Chelsey had woke up and came downstairs when she heard her grandma's voice. She stood there quietly, watching, waiting but not sure what she was waiting for.

"Yes, Ken was bringing Chelsey's new cat home when the accident happened."

Chelsey gasped which got her mother's and grandmother's attention.

"Come here, darlin'," Grace said and held out her arms, but her granddaughter turned and, with head hung low, went back up to her room.

"She's hurting," Grace said.

Capone meowed.

"Now I don't know what to do with Capone," Darla said.

"Have you fed him this morning?"

"No, he's been in the cage since the cops brought him home last night."

"Well, we better feed him. Where's the cat food?" Grace said, and Darla pointed to the kitchen cupboards. "I'll get his breakfast, you let him out of the cage," Grace said and stepped into the kitchen.

Darla bent down and looked at Capone. He looked frightened. She opened the carrier gate and Capone ran out, looking for a place to hide. He ran into the living room and out into the kitchen. He left the kitchen and went upstairs quickly until he found a place he hoped he wouldn't be found.

In the kitchen, Grace put out some Meow Mix and water. Darla came into the kitchen and told her mother where Capone went.

"He's scared because he's in a new home and everything. He'll come out eventually. Have you put out some litter for him?"

"We put it in the furnace room when Chelsey was at her friend's yesterday." Darla's lower lip and chin started to tremble, and Grace held her daughter again, knowing any mention of Ken is going to get her upset for a long time to come.

After a minute or two, Darla pulled away and said, "I'm alright. Mom. I'm alright. We should get the turkey in the oven. Ken's gone, but we're still having a Christmas dinner.

"Good," Grace said. "I'll call your dad and let him know."

- 2 -

Upstairs, Chelsey pushed her face into her pillow, crying. "Why did you die, Daddy? I want you back home. Please come home."

Chelsey didn't see Capone come into her room. He stayed low to the floor and ducked under the bed.

"God, please bring my daddy home."

She kicked all her stuffed animals off the bed and slammed her head back into the pillow. She stayed there sobbing until she felt something tickle her face. She opened her eyes and saw Capone's whiskers were touching her cheek. He was sniffing her, and his whiskers were wiggling.

Chelsey jumped up and yelled, "Get out of here, you stupid cat! You're the reason my daddy died. It's your fault. I wish I never saw you. Get out!"

Capone darted off the bed, ran out into the hallway, down the stairs, and hid behind the couch.

"I hate that cat."

Chapter Five

- 1 -

A few minutes after two, Chelsey's Grandpa Tom – a tall thin man who loved to dance – arrived and went to see his granddaughter upstairs in her room. He knocked on the door and gently opened it.

"Sweet Pea?" He always called her that.

Chelsey looked up, tears on her face, and almost shouted, " Grandpa." She got up off her bed and ran to him.

"My daddy's dead."

"I know," he said. They embraced without a sound. After a while, Tom wiped her tears away and looked her in the eye. "You need to be strong for your mom. She's hurting, too."

Chelsey nodded.

"C'mon, let's go downstairs. Your mom and grandma are cooking Christmas dinner and need our help." He thought it best she keep busy and maybe take her mind off her dad.

- 2 -

As soon as they reached the kitchen, Darla put Chelsey to work cutting carrots and then some celery.

Soon, more family arrived, many who had plans at their own homes but decided Darla and Chelsey needed them. Fifteen relatives in all came, most bringing food. They had enough food to serve thirty.

The home was bustling with people and conversation about Ken, saying he was a great guy, good husband and father. A family of cat lovers, soon the talk turned to cats.

"Ken loved cats. He got one for Chelsey for Christmas."

"Where is he?"

"Hiding. There's too much commotion going on in his new home. He's a little scared."

"The poor thing."

"What kind is he?"

"A Tuxie."

"Aww, they're so cute."

"Didn't Ken have an orange one? I love orange ones."

"Yea, Red. Did Ken ever tell you what he brought home one day?"

"A half-dead mouse?"

"No. Five and a half wieners."

"What? Really? How did he carry five wieners?"

"They figured he brought them home in his mouth one at a time from someone's garbage."

"I guess he figured he needed to feed his humans."

"Ken and Darla called him garbage guts."

"He was such a beautiful boy."

"I got a Siamese. And she brought home a dead gopher that looked like it got run over."

"Ewww." And they laughed.

"You know what Scottie, my big Tabby puss, does to me? He gets between whatever I'm reading and me. It's like he's saying, 'Pay attention to me.'"

"So does mine."

"And mine. But she's so cute I grab her and kiss her a whole bunch, and she quickly gets down."

Giggles.

"That wouldn't work with me. Scottie loves kisses – or at least he puts up with them."

"I love kissin' cats."

34

"Yea, well, a few days ago my Billy Puss stole a piece of my fish and chips before I sat down to eat."

"Did you get it back?"

"Nope, didn't bother. I wasn't going to eat it after he had his paws and teeth on it. Besides it hit the floor when he jumped down then he picked it up and ran down the hall."

Gasps and laughter.

The conversation ended when Chelsey entered the room.

"Dinner's ready," she said.

"Do you like your new cat?"

"No."

Silence.

And then they filed into the dining room. The lively conversation soon continued over dinner and afterward with pumpkin pie and Cool Whip for dessert.

Some relatives went home soon after supper, each hugging Darla and Chelsey and expressing condolences and Merry Christmases. Others helped with the clean up before they too went home. The last to leave were Chelsey's grandparents.

Darla and Chelsey sat in the living room, daughter on mother, and watched "Shrek the Halls" on DVD. Chelsey fell asleep, and Darla carried her upstairs, barely. The girl had grown.

After putting her daughter to bed, Darla went back downstairs and turned on Ken's favorite album – "Faith" by George Michael. She sat on the couch. The title song came on, and Darla asked, "What am I going to do without you?"

Then she heard some crunching coming from the kitchen. She got up off the couch to investigate, suspecting what it was. She turned on the kitchen light and saw Capone eating the cat food left out for him. And she smiled a little smile.

Chapter Six

Three days after Christmas, Darla sat her daughter down to explain the next day. She reached out to her daughter and took her hand.

"Chelsey, We're going to bury your father tomorrow. Do you know what happens at a funeral?"

Chelsey shook her head.

"There will be a casket with Daddy in it. It will be closed." She didn't explain his head was too mangled to have an open casket. "We will sit in the family area. The pastor will say a prayer and your Uncle Wesley will give the eulogy. That's where he talks about how good your dad was. Then your dad's favorite song will be played."

"You Make My Dreams?"

"Yes. When the service is over, we will go to the cemetery and bury him. You gonna be okay?"

Chelsey nodded and hugged her mom. "He was such a good daddy."

Behind them, Capone jumped onto the back of the couch. He stuck his nose between them and purred. Darla smiled and gave him a scratch around his ears.

"Mom, can we get rid of this cat?

Darla's mouth dropped open. "What? Why?"

"If not for that cat, Daddy would still be alive."

"Chelsey, it's not Capone's fault he's dead. It's the woman who was driving drunk. It's her fault."

"Yea, but if Daddy wasn't out getting that cat, he would still be alive. He'd be here – right now."

"It's not the cat's fault. I know you're mad, Honey, but you can't blame Capone."

"I don't want him here, I don't want him in my room, I don't want him at all. I hate cats."

"I know that's not true. You're hurt and angry. I understand, Honey. So am I. I want her to pay. She killed your daddy and hardly got hurt – just a few stitches."

"I hope the police got her too," Chelsey said. Then a moment of silence.

"You know, Sweetheart, getting Capone for you for Christmas was your dad's last gesture of love to you. He wanted you to have him, to love him. Look at him. He's so cute."

Chelsey looked at Capone and quietly said, "Stupid cat."

And Capone purred.

Chapter Seven

- 1 -

Sleepy-eyed and dopey, Chelsey got out of bed. Her father's funeral was today at 10am, and she had to get ready. She went into the bathroom, peed, and was glad she didn't see Capone. She turned on the bathroom radio and got undressed. The Wanted came over the airwaves. She loved The Wanted and this song, "Glad You Came," particularly. A bouncy tune. She needed that.

After turning on the shower, she got in and let the water run over her, wondering and hoping if this shower could go on forever. She didn't see Capone come into the bathroom. She shampooed her red hair and washed her freckled face and body. After rinsing off, she turned off the water, and slid open the shower door. She took a towel off the rack and put it on her head, rubbing her face and hair. She didn't see Capone approach.

Suddenly, she felt something wet and rough on her right foot. She pulled the towel off her head and looked down. Capone was licking her toes.

"Ewww! Gross! Go away! Mom! Mom!"

From her bedroom, Darla rushed into the bathroom to see what was going on. And laughed. "He's drying you off," she said.

"Please, Mom, make him stop."

Darla picked up Capone and held him.

"Stupid cat."

"He's just showing he loves you," Darla told her daughter. And her daughter let out a loud, hard, heavy sigh.

"Okay, get ready. I'm going to start making breakfast."

Darla left the bathroom with Capone, closing the door behind her. Chelsey finished drying herself off, took her blue housecoat from the hook on the door and put it on. She went downstairs to eat breakfast. It was 8:35am.

- 2 -

After the funeral, everyone agreed it was a beautiful ceremony. Many tears flowed, and they said good-bye to Kenneth Ashton. Ken's elderly parents made the four hour trip to attend and gave Ken's wife and daughter hugs and gentle words. The church was full of mourners offering condolences.

They buried Ken in the Langston Falls Cemetery with a short service. A luncheon in the church basement followed with much talk about Ken and plenty of finger food, coffee, and Tang. Eventually, most people filtered out, leaving a few to clean up the hall and turn out the lights. Darla and Chelsey went home sad yet satisfied.

One thing had been neglected, and it was time to take care of it.

- 3 -

They arrived home a little after one in the afternoon and decided to open their Christmas gifts. There would be some from Ken, but they would be strong. Darla and Chelsey kneeled around the old tree. They each took a turn opening a gift, leaving the ones from Ken last.

Chelsey got The Wanted "Battleground" CD she asked for and couldn't wait to import it onto her iPod. Clothes, including a purple blouse, for Chelsey – she looked cute in purple and loved the color – were given. Chelsey gave her mother a set of fancy soaps and bath salts that she bought by saving her allowance.

Darla picked up a small box that had a red ribbon on it. It was from Ken. A note attached said, "To My Darling Wife With All My Heart." Darla barely held back the tears.

"Open it, Mom."

She undid the ribbon, placed it aside, and opened the green box. Inside was a long gold chain with a sitting cat pendant and a small diamond for the eye.

"It's beautiful," she said, and Chelsey nodded. Darla put the chain around her neck, and Chelsey did up the clasp. Darla gazed at the pendant and ran her fingers over it.

Off to her right, Capone had come into the room and started playing with the ribbon. They watched as he flopped to the floor, bit the ribbon, and rolled around with it. Suddenly, he got up and raced out of the living room and up the stairs with the ribbon in his mouth and dragging behind him. Darla laughed. Chelsey did not. But she held back a smile that almost leaked out.

"He's such a funny kitty. And he's got that milk moustache I love. Isn't he cute?"

"No – maybe – I don't know," Chelsey said and shrugged.

All the gifts to Darla and Chelsey were opened. The ones for Ken remained unopened. Darla decided to return the gifts to the store. They would need the money until his life insurance check arrived. It was a $200,000 policy, but she would take him back without the money if she could.

Chelsey had about a week until school started again, and Darla decided to wait to return to work at Co-op Grocery Store until then. She needed time for both of them.

Chapter Eight

- 1 -

Darla dropped Chelsey off at Webster Niblock School the morning classes started again after Christmas holidays and headed for work for her first day back as well.

After Chelsey got out of the car, Sue ran up and hugged her. The two friends hadn't seen each other since before Christmas.

"Good morning, Darla," Sue yelled after Darla had already driven away. She turned back to Chelsey.

"I'm sorry about your dad," she said and hugged Chelsey again.

"What did you get for Christmas?" Chelsey asked, wanting to change the subject.

"I got a new Barbie. I love Barbie. And a Barbie car too. New jeans and this shirt I got on. Look." Sue opened her jacket, revealing a pink shirt with a picture of her cat on it.

Chelsey looked and said, "Cool" but didn't mean it.

"My grandma gave me fifty dollars. Mom says I can spend twenty dollars, and the rest goes in the bank. We went to see her in Calgary for Christmas. We went to the Calgary Tower. Oh, and I got this Mickey Mouse watch. I love it." Sue showed her watch to Chelsey. "I love it, too."

"What did you get?" Sue asked. Chelsey listed what she got for Christmas and ended with, "And a cat I don't want."

"You got that cat?" That's so cool."

"No, it's not. You want him?"

"Really?"

Chelsey nodded.

"Yeah, I'll take him." Sue jumped up and down a few times. "I already got one cat. I love cats. Did you name him 'Suits'?"

"No. I don't want to name him. I'll bring him over tomorrow."

"Okay, but I gotta ask my mom first."

The bell rang signaling school's starting, and the girls ran inside.

- 2 -

Outside after school, it snowed. The girls walked together until they had to part ways to get home.

"Don't forget to ask your mom," Chelsey said while walking away from her friend.

"I won't. Bye."

"Bye."

Chelsey walked alone, getting home a little before four. Her mother was home from the grocery store, sitting at the kitchen table, holding an envelope. Darla knew what was inside. A check for $200,000.00. The money would pay for Ken's funeral, the remainder of the mortgage, and the $26,783.27 in credit card debt they accumulated over the years. That would leave about $15,000.00. Darla decided it would go into a college fund for Chelsey they always meant to start. The phone rang. Darla answered it.

"Hello?"

"Hello, Dar. It's Liz, Sue's mom. I thought you should know Chelsey offered to give her new cat to Sue today. With Ken being gone, I wanted to be sure she's not giving him away and then wanting him back later when she's feeling, well, better. I mean, we'll take him if you're giving him away."

"No, we're not giving Capone away. You're right. Chelsey's having a hard time since Ken's death. I'm hoping she'll warm up to Capone."

"Fine, bye." Liz hung up without waiting for Darla to say goodbye. Darla hung up the phone.

She called her daughter into the kitchen and explained that they were keeping Capone.

"He's my cat. Dad gave him to me so I can do whatever I want with him, and I want to give him to Sue."

"Don't get that way with me, young lady. Capone's a part of this family now so you better get used to having him here. Got it?"

Chelsey crossed her arms and went silent.

"Chelsey, do you get it? Chelsey?" Darla raised her voice to her daughter. "Do you get it?"

"Fine," Chelsey said and stomped up to her room where she stayed until she got hungry.

Darla wanted Chelsey to love Capone but knew she some work ahead of her.

Chapter Nine

Good Friday came and went with Darla and Chelsey attending church as they had every year. Soon Easter Sunday arrived, and the Easter Bunny delivered gifts. Chelsey hunted around their home for her gifts. She found milk chocolate eggs, a white chocolate bunny, a DVD of Disney's *That Darn Cat*.

"What is this?" Chelsey asked holding up the DVD.

"*That Darn Cat*. I loved that movie when I was a kid. Come on, let's watch it," Darla said with a smile.

"But it's an old movie. I hate old movies." Darla knew the real reason she didn't want to watch it – because of the cat. Which is why Darla got it for her, hoping the cat would melt her heart.

"I'll let you eat your chocolate bunny if you watch it with me."

"Mmm – okay."

Chelsey unwrapped the DVD and put it in the DVD player. She picked up her chocolate bunny and sat on the couch and opened the plastic bag holding the white treat. The DVD started automatically. Capone joined them, lying on the back of the couch.

They watched the previews and soon D.C. – Darn Cat – was on the screen. A Seal Point Siamese boy, D.C. stole the show.

"Aww, he's so beautiful," Darla said and looked over at her daughter who was watching and eating but gave no reaction. Darla laughed at D.C. trying to get some fish, and Chelsey smiled.

Darla could tell her daughter – the cat hater – liked D.C. They laughed together when D.C. fought for the duck he stole. And the laughter kept coming.

For the entire movie, Capone slept and groomed himself on the back of the couch. Darla reached up and scratched him from time to time. The movie ended.

"What did you think? D.C.'s funny, isn't he?"

"Yea and cute too."

Darla smiled and said, "I got an Easter present for Capone."

Darla got up and went into the kitchen and returned with a bag of green catnip. "Watch this." She put some of the catnip on the carpet.

"Now put Capone down by the catnip." Chelsey reached up to the back of the couch, picked up Capone, and put him on the rug by the catnip.

Capone sniffed and rolled onto the rug and into the catnip. He stretched his paws out and pushed his face into the floor. He got up and ran in a circle around the nip. And Chelsey laughed.

He ran out of the living room and back in with his back arched. He rotated his head around and rolled back into the catnip.

"That cat's crazy," Chelsey said and laughed some more.

Chapter Ten

- 1 -

It was 8am when Darla came into the kitchen and heard a talkative Capone meowing for his breakfast. Darla measured out a quarter cup of Cat Chow and poured it into his dish. Capone quickly ate his breakfast while Darla cleaned and refilled his water bowl.

"Sheesh, cat. It's like you're starving to death." Capone loved to eat. It seemed he was always hungry. Capone finished his meal and spent a few minutes licking his chops.

Chelsey came into the kitchen, smelling of shampoo. She bent down and scratched Capone, and he leaned into her hand. She sat at the table to eat. Darla served her waffles and blueberries – her favorite breakfast. It was June 24th – six months since Ken died – and she didn't want her daughter thinking about it.

Chelsey finished her breakfast. Darla didn't feel like eating but ate anyway. After their meal, they got ready and were soon out the door to Webster Niblock School. Darla dropped Chelsey off and returned home. It was her day off, and she knew she would be thinking about her husband all day.

She turned on the t.v. and watched the morning news, hoping to take her mind off Ken. It didn't work. She burst out into tears.

Capone came into the living room and hopped onto the couch. He put both front paws on her leg and stuck his face into her's. She stopped crying, giving a little laugh. She gathered the cat into her arms and pushed her wet face into his soft fur. Capone purred. Darla felt better. Capone was a gift for daughter and mother.

- 2 -

After school, Chelsey went over to Sue's house with her mother's permission and on the condition she be home for supper. Darla figured Chelsey didn't notice that six months had past since her dad was killed.

In the living room, sunshine pierced the window and made a warm glow on the carpet that Capone basked in. As the sunlight moved across the rug so did Capone, staying warm.

Chelsey arrived home a few minutes before Darla started making supper. She made one of her daughter's favorites – teriyaki chicken wings, roasted garlic mashed potatoes, and peaches and cream corn.

After supper, Chelsey asked to watch *That Darn Cat* again. Darla said, "Okay." Soon they were laughing at D.C. again. When the movie was over, it was bedtime for Chelsey. She went upstairs, brushed her teeth, and changed into a nighty. She said a prayer, hoping God would help the sadness go away. Darla watched and listened at Chelsey's bedroom doorway. Chelsey got into bed, and Darla tucked her in and said, "Good night," with a kiss.

"Mom, why did Daddy have to die?"

"I don't know, Honey." Darla turned out the light. She started to close the door when Chelsey said, "No, leave it open. In case Capone wants to come in."

"Okay." Darla left the door slightly ajar.

Darla went downstairs and called her mother. They talked until Darla was ready for bed herself. Darla hung up the phone, turned off the lights, and went upstairs. She decided to check on

Chelsey. She found her sleeping in the fetal position with her left arm around Capone. Darla went to bed happy.

Chapter Eleven

- 1 -

Chelsey's tenth birthday came on September 14th. She expected a happy time and wasn't disappointed. Several friends, including Sue, came to Chelsey's birthday party. They brought gifts and got birthday cake, games, and Capone.

After some cake and Twister, the girls vacated the living room and went up to Chelsey's bedroom, dragging Capone with them. They put Capone on the bed, scratching and petting him. He loved the attention. Chelsey and her friends joined Capone on the bed.

"He's so cute," Jill said. "What's his name?"

"Capone," said Chelsey.

"I thought you were gonna name him 'Suits'?" Sue asked.

"No. I like Capone better. Suits him." And the girls laughed.

"Does he do any tricks?" Jill asked.

"Cats don't do tricks," Sue said.

"Capone does," Chelsey said, picking up Capone.

She put him on the floor and stood facing the black and white cat. Chelsey tapped her chest and said, "Up, Capone. Up, Capone."

Capone looked up at her with a blank expression.

"Up, Capone." She tapped her chest again. "I don't know why he's not doing –"

Suddenly Capone jumped into Chelsey's arms. The girls "oohed" and laughed. They got up and petted Capone some more and settled back on the bed.

"Where did you get him?" Jill asked.

"I got him for Christmas. I wish I didn't."

"But he's so beautiful," Jill said. "Why wouldn't you want him?"

"Cause her dad died," Sue said.

A few moments of silence was followed by Jill saying, "I like Paul Jacobson."

"Eww, gross," Chelsey said.

The girls talked about other boys – who was cute and who wasn't. And the giggling started.

They giggled and talked until each girl's parents showed up and took them home. Sue was the last to leave, wishing her best friend a happy birthday.

- 2 -

Darla came out of the kitchen where she had been cleaning up after the cake and said good-bye to each girl as she left. When Sue was gone, Chelsey turned to her mother and hugged her saying, "Best party ever!"

Darla laughed and hugged her back. A few glowing moments later Darla said, "C'mon, let's go finish cleaning the kitchen."

They stepped into the kitchen and found Capone on the counter with his head in the icing bowl, licking the sweet stuff. Both of them laughed and said, "Capone!" together.

Darla clapped her hands together several times and said, "Get down. Cats should not have people food. Or be on the counter. Get down." Capone ran off the counter, went to his food dish and meowed.

"Hungry kitty," Chelsey said. "Can I feed him?"

"Yea."

And Chelsey fed her cat, her Capone.

Chapter Twelve

- 1 -

It was mid-afternoon when Darla came into the house. She closed the front door, and leaned her back against the door.

"Oh, God," she said. "How could they?"

She slammed her fist into the door. She slid down to the floor and slammed her hand several more times until it hurt. She sat on the floor and screamed a raging scream.

"How could they?"

She wanted to swear and curse them to Hell – especially her. Tears began to flow – angry, bitter tears. Just how much was Ken's life worth?

After ten minutes, she let out a rumble from her throat and got up. She saw Capone hiding behind the couch, and she realized her banging and screaming frightened him. She took a deep breath and called her mother. She told her what happened. They spoke for 25 minutes with her mother reassuring her that it will work out. But Darla had doubts.

Darla hung up and started making supper. It would be an early meal, but she needed something to do to keep herself busy so she wouldn't think about it. Chelsey would be home soon.

When Chelsey got home, her mother called her into the kitchen and hugged her longer than usual.

"I love you, Mom."

She needed to hear that and decided to tell Chelsey after supper. The tuna casserole was ready 20 minutes later, and they ate. It was a good meal with ice cream and sundae sauce for dessert. Then they cleaned up. It was time to tell her daughter what happened.

Darla took Chelsey and sat her down on the couch. "I have to tell you something, Honey. I went to court today to see what would happen to the woman who killed your father. The defense and prosecutor made a deal that she would spend only three years in jail if she pled 'guilty.' Do you know what that means?"

Chelsey nodded, but Darla could tell she was a little confused.

"Because of our legal system, she only has to spend one-third of her sentence in prison. So she only got one whole year in jail." Talking about it brought back the angry tears.

"Why? Why did they do that? She should be in jail forever. Her whole life," Chelsey said through angry tears of her own.

"Murderers get life in prison. She was driving drunk and didn't care who she hurt that night." Darla took a breath and sighed. "It was her first offense, and she showed remorse so they let her get away with it."

"She got away with murder," Chelsey said. "I don't like those people."

"Drunk driving or murder. Ken's still dead."

They sat in silence and then hugged some more. After a while, Darla turned on the t.v. "Friends" was playing. It was an early episode. They watched it but didn't laugh.

Darla got up and found Capone curled up on a kitchen table chair. She reached under the table and pulled him out and carried him out to the living room. She handed the Tuxedo Cat to her child who hugged and held him, burying her face into his fur. Something about Capone made them both feel better.

Chapter Thirteen

- 1 -

December 24th came and so did the worst ice storm in the small city's history. The storm rained freezing drops early in the morning, coating everything from sidewalks to roads to power lines. Some power lines broke apart from the weight of the heavy ice coating and some were taken down by tree branches that broke off after being weighted down by the ice. Massive power outages resulted throughout Langston Falls. Luckily, Darla and Chelsey's power stayed on keeping them warm as the temperatures outside dropped. The freezing rain stopped, and the snow started.

One year had past since Kenneth Ashton, loving husband and father, died.

- 2 -

Winds picked up in the afternoon, blowing the snow around, and causing high snowdrifts and whiteout conditions. Darla and Chelsey watched the snowstorm through their living room window and knew they were not able to go to Ken's gravesite that day as planned.

Darla turned on the radio. "Heavy amounts of snow are expected overnight and into Christmas Day. The mayor and police are advising everyone to stay in their homes and only travel when absolutely necessary. We are expecting 12 to 25 inches of snow in some areas. If you can, hunker down where you are. The storm, which unexpectedly turned south into the city, is expected to clear late tomorrow morning, and then the clean up can begin. For those of you without power, city crews will be out restoring power as soon as possible, but it may take several days until all power is restored. Stay warm and safe," the disc jockey said. Darla turned off the radio and put an Elvis Christmas CD into the player.

"Let's decorate the tree," she said.

They had bought and brought home a Christmas tree the day before.

"It's a good tree," Chelsey said, clapped her hands, and laughed.

They went downstairs and brought up the cardboard box of old decorations. "Blue Christmas" played. Capone watched them with his golden eyes wide as they unpacked the decorations. Soon, he was trying to play with the shiny ornaments. They laughed.

In a short time, the old decorations were on the tree with none on the lower branches.

"It's missing something," Darla said.

"What? The star is up on top. All the decorations are on the tree. Did we miss some?" Chelsey said and looked in the cardboard box.

Darla smiled and pulled out a bag from behind the couch and handed it to her daughter. Chelsey grabbed it and peered inside. She found new decorations – twelve white and purple ornaments.

"They're beautiful," Chelsey said. "Can we put them on the tree?" Darla nodded. Carefully, Chelsey hung each new glass ball on the green artificial tree.

The decorating was done, and the two ladies stood back and admired their work.

"It looks great," Darla said.

"Dad would have loved it."

They watched Capone approach and lay down on the skirt beneath the tree. And they smiled.

"He wants to be a Christmas present," Chelsey said.

"He's a gift alright."

Dinnertime came, and they sat down to a chicken dinner. A small ham was waiting in the fridge for Christmas Day.

The weather was frigid and temperatures continued to drop. The snow came down heavily, stopping everything in Langston Falls. They were snowed in. Minus twenty was the temperature outside when the power went out in the Ashton home. No power – no heat.

"Oh no," Darla said when the lights went out. The sun was already down so it got dark in their home.

"I'm scared, Mom."

A single light from an emergency flashlight lit the kitchen. Darla got some candles and set them alight. Knowing the power could be out for days, Darla and Chelsey got out extra blankets and brought the candles into the living room. They cuddled together on the couch under the blankets. It got cold fast, and Darla wished she had better insulation in her home.

To take their minds off the cold, mother and daughter talked about anything but the cold. Soon, the conversation turned to Capone.

"Where is he?" Chelsey asked and looked about but couldn't see him.

"I'm sure he'll make an appearance soon," her mother said.

"Mom." She paused. "I know I hated him at first. I'm sorry."

"Aww, Honey. You were angry about your dad dying. That's a lot for a nine year old to deal with. How do you feel about him now?"

"I love him," she said quickly. "He's so cute." And her mother gave her a squeeze. "I love it when he runs around the house for no reason."

"And he's as loud as a herd of elephants."

"Yea. And I let him lick my feet when I get out of the shower now."

"He's a funny kitty."

"He loves that mouse on a string we got him. It's so funny when bats it out of the air and then bites it and then runs away and runs back and bats it again."

"I love his purr. He's a loud purrer. I like to hold his throat to my ear and listen to him purr. You know, some cats hate to be kissed, but Capone just sits there and lets you kiss him –"

"Lots," Chelsey added. "I like to kiss his milk moustache, over and over."

The temperature dropped some more – enough that their noses got cold. Darla lit some more candles, hoping the heat from the flame would help keep them warm. They started to see the breath leave their mouths.

It was getting late. Chelsey fell asleep in her mother's arms, something she hadn't done since she was a little girl. Darla prayed.

"Lord, Jesus. Please see us through this cold night. Please keep us safe and warm."

Eventually, Darla also fell asleep, wondering if they would survive the night. And it got colder.

- 4 -

The next morning the sun rose lighting the Ashton living room. Darla woke up and found her daughter still breathing, and Capone curled up on their laps. He had kept them warm through the cold night.

"Thank you, Jesus," Darla whispered not wanting to wake her daughter.

The power came back on three hours later. Darla and Chelsey survived the worst winter storm in Langston Falls history. Christmas had arrived, and they celebrated – opening gifts, hugging and kissing, eating Christmas dinner, loving the day. And Capone too.

60

Chapter Fourteen

- 1 -

By the time New Years Day came around, all the snow had been removed and all power restored to the city. The Parkers, the Ashton's neighbors, used their new snow blower to clean off Darla's sidewalks and driveway. Appreciative, Darla gave them a box of Turtles chocolates. Now they could visit Ken.

- 2 -

The air was a little below freezing when Ken's wife and daughter stood at his gravesite. Darla laid flowers on his headstone. The headstone read: " Beloved Husband and Father."

Darla told him what had happened since he died and hoped he could hear her in Heaven. Chelsey stood by quietly and listen to her mother.

"I love you and miss you," they each said.

They turned to leave when Chelsey turned back and said, "Daddy, thank you for Capone. He's the best gift ever." And they went home.

Darla and Chelsey would always remember Ken as a wonderful husband and father as their lives went on. Darla would eventually remarry a man from church, and Chelsey grew up to become a beautiful young woman. Capone lived to a healthy 18 years. And when they buried him, they thought of the man who brought this special cat into their lives. Never forgetting either of them.

The Christmas Cat 3

Chapter One

The cold pulled at his body heat when he stepped outside his motel room door. The weather app on his iPhone revealed a -35 degree temperature with a wind chill of -47 degrees. Just the way he wanted it.

He walked to the stairs of the Sunrise Motel and stepped down to the ground floor. The freezing temperature drew warmth from his body. He'd left his winter coat in his room, and he felt it. He'd shaved off his beard so the cold could freeze his face.

Good, he thought. *I don't deserve to be warm.*

Walking out of the motel parking lot, Alan went toward the highway where no buildings could shield him from the bitter winds. Goosebumps appeared and disappeared on his skin as his body tried to get warm. The winds blew up and cut him to the bone. He wondered how long it will take him to die. He wore a t-shirt, jeans and runners so he could freeze faster.

This winter had been hell, and he knew he'd be there soon. His muscles tightened. He shivered. Five minutes past since he'd gone out to die.

Snow crunched beneath his feet as he passed through an open field by the highway. He stopped and looked up.

"Why did you do this to me?" he said.

His mind and body wanted him to cross his arms to conserve heat, but the part that wanted him to die was stronger. He left his arms at his sides. The frigid gusts ravaged him and ripped out his warmth. Hypothermia started to set in.

Death would happen soon, he knew it. He welcomed it. The cold burnt him – his arms, his face, his fingers, his back, his soul. He shook.

Alan drew close to the highway, and considered ending it by being hit by a semi-truck as a quicker way to finish it. No, he wanted a slow death.

He came to the highway ditch and watched the few cars out this dark night speed past.

He heard a "meow." A light, soft, barely audible meow. Alan hadn't heard such a meow before. It sounded like a kitten, and he looked into the ditch. A small ball of matted fur approached him. She meowed again.

Looks like a Ragdoll.

He stepped down with a slight stumble into the ditch where the temperature felt a few degrees warmer and the wind blew over the top. He reached the kitten and picked her up.

She feels so cold. Who would leave a kitten out on a night like this?

She cuddled into him. She shivered and shook and so did Alan. He knew if he died this night, so would she. He wrapped both arms around her and climbed out of the ditch. He had to get her out of this glacial weather as fast as he could. It meant her life.

He moved as quickly as he could across the field back toward the motel. The conditions slowed him down. The subzero winds let up. He wanted to run but knew that would create a wind chill as he hurried through the cold air. Alan trudged through the snow not going as fast as he knew he had to. She needed him. He needed to get her warm.

The winds picked up again, blowing across his back. The extreme winter temperatures dug deep into him. He had never felt so cold.

He reached the edge of the field and stepped onto the motel parking lot. Almost there. The kitten didn't move. Alan didn't want to pull his arms from her to check on her because the chill would get at her.

They arrived. He took her up the stairs, each step a struggle, his legs freezing. They got up to his room. Suddenly, he realized he didn't bring his keycard with him. They were locked out. The front desk closed for the holiday. They needed to get inside now or freeze to death.

"Oh, God."

Alan kicked the door and it flew open. He hadn't latched it. In his haste to die, he hadn't cared if the door closed all the way.

Inside they went. He put the Ragdoll kitten on the bed and covered her with a blanket. She breathed.

"Thank God."

He smiled his first smile in weeks.

Alan turned the heat up to high. They both needed to get warm fast. He took another blanket and shivered as he wrapped himself in it. He curled up on the bed and watched his new kitten. He decided not to find out whose cat she was – if she had an owner. Any good person would not leave her out in this weather.

Man and cat warmed up. After a while, he turned on the t.v. *It's a Wonderful Life* had started a few minutes before. He had never seen this old black and white movie, but it may add color to his life.

When the part where Clarence, the angel trying to earn his wings, jumped into the water to save George from himself, Alan felt something soft. The kitten had come out of the blanket and found a spot to curl up next to him. She was warm. He ran his fingers through her fur. She had some mats. She purred. He had warmed up too.

"I'm hungry. And I bet you are too."

He didn't want to disturb his new feline, but his leftover tuna sandwich sat in the mini-fridge across the room. He picked her up and placed her back on the bed. She meowed a little.

He got to the fridge and retrieved to half-eaten sandwich. He returned to the bed and put the sub beside her. She showed a quick and intense interest in the meal. She sniffed the plastic wrap and tried to bite through to the tuna.

"Hold on, hold on. Boy, you must be hungry. When was the last time you ate?"

He ran his hand over her. He could tell she was underweight. He pulled open the wrap and took out the sandwich. She tried to paw it out of his hand. So he took some tuna out of the sub and set it on the bed. She ate it immediately. And came for more. He scooped out the rest of the fish and gave it to her. And down it went.

After Alan ate the rest of the sandwich, the small ball of fluff found comfort in Alan's lap. He continued watching the movie. In the classic film, George wanted to kill himself after his life fell apart. Just like Alan. An angel without wings saved George. Alan looked down at his new friend.

"Are you my angel with no wings?"

He petted the small cat and touched her warmth. He became warmer. He noticed the many mats in her fur and took one in his fingers. She mewed in pain.

"We'll have to do something about those mats. But I want to watch my movie first."

When the film finished, he threw the blanket off and got up. He got the clippers he'd used to shave off his beard and a comb and returned to the bed. He sat down beside the young feline and located a large mat. Taking the comb, he pulled the mat away from her skin. Using the clippers, he shaved the mat off. A slow but necessary process.

The kitten sat still and allowed Alan to care for her. When he finished removing all her clumps of fur, he held her up and gave her the once over. She now had bald spots and her fur appeared dirty.

"Time to give you a bath."

Alan got off the bed and deposited the removed mats into the bathroom garbage. He opened the shower curtain and turned on the water. After a few seconds, warm water flowed over his fingers. A good feeling. He wanted to get in the tub because he hadn't bathed in three days. But she came first.

He filled the water up halfway and fetched some shampoo. The mini-motel bottle would have to do. He got his Ragdoll and placed her in the water. Much to his surprise, she didn't resist or try to scramble out.

"What a good kitty, you are. How could some jerk leave you outside to die?"

He washed and rinsed her and pulled the plug. Picking her up, he checked her rear end and wrapped her in a towel.

"So you're a girl. I suspected as much."

Even though they were in a warm room, she could still get cold with wet fur in the winter. The colder it is, the more it creeps in. He had to get her dry. Alan rubbed his new puss with a towel and used a blow dryer to finish the job. And then he laughed. He hadn't laughed since the breakup. Her fur had fluffed out from the blow-drying.

"You're so cute with your fur poofed out like that. I think I'll call you 'Poof.' Yep, that's your name: Poof."

The clock/radio said 12:13am.

"Merry Christmas, Poof," he said and kissed her on the head. He scratched her back.

His head itched and he knew why. He needed to shower. He smelt his armpits and his face soured.

Yep, I need to get clean.

He undressed and showered. He let the hot water warm him. The hypothermia left him. He was warm inside and out. He washed and turned off the water. After drying off, he got into bed. He picked up Poof and laid her on his chest. He drifted off, falling asleep scratching her. He now knew life was more than what that woman put him through. His Christmas cat taught him that.

Chapter Two

Alan met Kimberly two years before in a bar in Oshawa. He loved her good looks, and she loved his earning power. He learned that a few days before he walked out into the cold to die.

Being a grocery store supervisor didn't make him rich, but he had saved enough to buy his first home. He had worked hard to pay off his credit card debt and rebuild his credit rating. In a few more months, he would be ready to purchase a modest home. A good start. Then he met her.

She showered attention on him. Smiling at him, touching his arm and face, and gazing into his eyes like no woman had done before.

Alan struggled in the dating world. Having only a few short-lived love relationships before Kim – the longest lasting four months. Long and wide gaps sat between girlfriends.

Alan – a plain, average, short man with a pot belly – did not fancy women's dream dates. So when he met Kim, a dream had come true. The dream started on a bar stool. Alan sat alone at the bar, sipping a draft beer when she sat beside him.

"Hi," she said. "Who are you?"

Their conversation didn't stop until they had to leave at closing time. She wanted to know everything about him. And he told her, even his plans to buy a house. He loved her attention.

Kim wrote down her cell number and told him to call her. Excited, Alan said he would.

He watched her walk away. She turned and smiled and blew him a kiss. Alan could see good things to come with her. His heart pounded hard. His body felt light, like on air.

When Alan got home that night, Buster welcomed him home with loud meowing to get fed. He lifted up his orange and white tomcat and hugged and kissed him.

"I met a girl tonight, Buster."

Buster jumped down and ran to his dish and meowed. He hadn't been fed since the morning.

"Are you hungry?"

Buster continued meowing and walked about his dish with his back arched and his tail straight up. Alan fed his boy Whiskas dry cat food. He watched his feline eat and smiled a big smile.

Life is good.

But it was about to change.

*

Alan and Kim dated and he fell in love. He wanted to give her everything. A wonderful affair grew between them until she said, "I'm not happy here. I want to go back to Langston Falls. That's my home. I want you to come, but you have to find a new home for your cat."

"But I love Buster," he said to her.

"Either me or that cat," she said to him.

They argued over Buster until she told him she missed her family in Langston Falls, and she would be returning home there with or without him.

"If you love me, you'll get rid of that cat and come with me. Cats are vile creatures. I hate them. Hate them. So, what is it? Me or him?"

The ache of leaving Buster behind weighed on him when he said, "I'll find him a nice home." And he did with a pain in his heart. He would also be leaving his family and friends he knew he would miss them dearly – especially his mother.

*

70

When moving day came, Kim told him he needed to pay her last month's rent and the moving expenses. She also had him settle her utility and cable bills which were months behind.

They arrived in Langston Falls in the spring, renting an apartment together. Kim introduced him to her family - mother, father and sister – and all seemed fine. But Kim always seemed broke and wanted money.

She asked him to get her a credit card in his name that she could use because she needed to get a few things for their new home together. In *his* name because her credit wasn't so good or so she told him. She promised to only use the credit card for necessaries and emergencies. And just to be on the safe side, she needed a high credit limit. Alan agreed. Anything for her. Soon, Alan applied for three more credit cards.

Alan found work at a local Safeway grocery store. She refused to work.

"The man works," she said.

He paid all the bills. When she asked to put his bank account in both their names, he did. For her birthday, she demanded a nice new car. Alan took out a car loan for a new Toyota Camry with the title in her name and the loan in his.

Kim started to disappear. After Alan finished the late shift at the grocery store, he would find she wasn't home.

Where is she?

When she would get home in the early of hours of the morning, she reeked of alcohol, her hair and clothes a mess and with the excuse of going out with the girls. Several times she went missing for two or three days with no explanation.

"What is going on?" he asked her.

"Nothing's going on," she answered.

Sleep became difficult for Alan. Being tired all the time wore him down. His work at the store suffered so much they fired him. He told Kim he'd been let go.

"Well, you're no good to me anymore," she said. "I'm leaving. You're useless. I have another man anyway. Get out."

Alan packed a backpack with a few things and left without a word.

What an idiot I am. I should have seen it, he thought.

71

He called his four credit card companies and found all his cards maxed out. He had a little bit left on his MasterCard. He owed over $26,000.00 in credit card debt. All in his name.

He visited his bank to take her off his savings and chequing accounts and found them almost empty. His $38,000.00 he had saved for a house gone. He checked the balance of his car loan for *her* car and found he owed over $22,000.00.

Destitute, his debt totaled $49,730.59, he had no job and little money. He'd lost the only woman he had ever loved to another man. She had taken everything from him. Christmas was three days away.

Alan checked into the Sunrise Motel with the last bit of credit he had on his MasterCard. He felt the fool. He had no way of getting back to Oshawa. He had left his family, his friends and his Buster to move out west with *that* woman. He wanted to evaporate into nothing.

She had never loved him and put him on the road to bankruptcy. But what could he do? He raged and cried for two days. He ate little. He wanted to drown himself in alcohol but didn't have any way of buying even one bottle. He didn't call anyone. Shame plagued him. No one must know the idiot he became. He wanted to die.

And on Christmas Eve, he walked out into a deadly freeze and found life. Life in the shape of a small Ragdoll kitten named Poof.

Chapter Three

Christmas morning he woke to find Poof by his side. He laid in bed and thought. He had to get his life in order.

He turned on the t.v. and found Christmas cartoons playing. He threw off the covers. Poof meowed in protest. She wanted him to stay in bed, Alan believed. But he needed to get up and get on with his life. What could be done on this day? He got up, peed and showered. When he dried himself off, Poof stuck her head into the bathroom and mewed.

"Are you hungry? Well, so am I."

He put on clean underwear. At least, he had that. He searched the mini-fridge, hoping for something but found nothing. They had finished off the tuna sandwich last night. He sighed.

"Nothing we can do on Christmas Day. Just starve through it and look for a job tomorrow."

Poof mewed some more.

"Sorry, Poof. I can't feed – you don't have any water. And I don't have a bowl."

Alan fished out the tuna sandwich wrapper and formed it into a bowl. He filled it with water. As soon as he put it down, she drank – lots.

"Sorry, furry kitty. I never though of water."

Alan heard bells – big bells, church bells. He went to the window and drew the curtain. He scanned the scene outside his room and saw a cross high above the other buildings on a steeple.

"Poof, I'm going to church."

Chapter Four

"I haven't been to church since I was a kid, Poof," Alan said and gave her a scratch that she pushed into, turning her head around. He got dressed and put his runners and winter coat on. He left his motel room with hope.

He walked toward the church steeple with the wind blowing cold. He pushed his hands into his pockets and put his head down. Even with his coat on, he froze.

Five minutes later, he rounded a corner and discovered the church – a large, beautiful building with many windows and the tall steeple Alan had followed. The church parking lot looked full. Alan crossed the street, went between the vehicles and entered the house of prayer. Heat – glorious heat – enveloped him. A man dressed in a suit approached.

"Are you new to the church?" the man said. "I haven't seen you before."

Alan nodded and shook the man's hand.

"I'm Paul."

"Alan. May I see the pastor?"

"Of course," Paul said and turned to show Alan the way to the pews.

"He just got started. There's room at the back."

Alan opened the door to the chapel and went in. He found a seat in the close to capacity congregation. He sat and listened to the pastor speak.

"I received a letter from a woman I'll call Betty – that's not her real name. She wrote that she had not forgiven when she had the chance. You see, her husband of 43 years had had an affair early in their marriage. She didn't know about the affair. But when he found out he had terminal brain cancer and only had a month to live, he confessed to her. Obviously, this upset her. He asked her to forgive him. She refused. On his deathbed, he asked her again to forgive him and again she refused. He died without her forgiveness.

"In the letter, Betty describes the agony she feels five years after his death. She is no longer angry with him for having the affair. No, she is in pain because she did not forgive him when she had the chance. She let that chance slip away. And now at 83, she is slipping away heavy with the guilt of not forgiving her husband.

"Jesus taught us to forgive as he forgave. Do you have a relative or friend or even a stranger who has done you wrong that you have not forgiven?

"Families come together at this time of Christ's birth. Some of your family may be in need of forgiveness. Do not allow this holiday of forgiveness to go by without forgiving those who have wronged us.

"If you are in need of forgiveness, ask for it. Tell them you wronged them and that you need their forgiveness. This is the season of love and joy and charity. Please extended the season into forgiveness."

Alan wondered if he could forgive Kim. He certainly wouldn't be doing it anytime soon.

Alan's attention drifted off the pastor and his sermon. He gazed about the room at the backs of people's heads. He saw blonde, brown and black hair. Two redheads caught his attention. They stood out with their beautiful hair, each pulled back into a ponytail.

Little girls, probably sisters. Twins?

Beside them sat a tall man with salt and pepper hair.

Probably their dad.

The parishioners sang a hymn, and the sermon ended with the pastor reminding everyone about the Christmas charity supper that afternoon. He left the pulpit and headed to the front exit. The crowd filed toward the door where Pastor Jim thanked each man, woman and child for attending and wished each a "Merry Christmas."

Alan waited until they had all left and then approached the pastor.

"I need your help," he said.

Chapter Five

Jim smiled at him. He introduced himself and shook Alan's hand.

"What's going on, Alan?"

"I tried to kill myself last night."

"I see. How do you feel now?"

"Relieved. I don't want to die anymore."

"Good."

"But I do need your help. I've lost everything. My job, my money and the woman I thought loved me."

Alan's lip quivered and tears wet his eyes. Jim put his hand on Alan's shoulder.

"Come," Jim said. "Let's sit down. Do you want to talk about it?"

"Yes."

The two men sat in the pews. Alan explained, telling Jim about Kim and how she took him by pretending to be in love with him.

"Do you still love her?"

"I think so. It's hard to let go of those feelings."

"But you know she isn't for you."

"Yes, of course."

Alan told him about his attempt to freeze himself to death and how Poof saved his life just by being there.

"A gift from God, no doubt," Jim said. "You saved her too."

"A gift from God, alright. But I have no food to feed her or myself, for that matter."

"We are having a community Christmas dinner at four for those down on their luck or need to be in the company of others on this holiday. Please join us."

Alan hungered now, and he was sure Poof did too. But he didn't want to impose anymore than he already had. He would wait for the dinner and take food back for Poof afterwards.

"Thanks. I'll be there," Alan said.

However, Alan did not tell Jim his credit cards were useless and he only had one night left at the motel and then he and his kitten would be homeless tomorrow.

One thing at a time.

He said, "Goodbye, Jim," and walked out the doors.

Chapter Six

Alan returned to the motel and got welcomed with a loud meow. She wanted to be fed. So did he. But they had nothing until supper.

"I'll bring you some turkey later."

He took off his coat and shoes and dropped onto the bed. With remote control in hand, he flipped channels until he found an old black and white movie. He watched *A Christmas Carol* and wished he'd been more like Scrooge – stingy.

"Lesson learned," he said.

The movie ended. He wanted to call his mother in Oshawa didn't want to worry her. Besides he couldn't pay for the call. He would call her when and if he could get back on his feet and heading back to Oshawa. She hated her son being away from her. He longed for Oshawa. His home. When he had the money, he'd leave this rotten town as fast as he could. He had no reason to stay here. He would take Poof and go home. Alan looked up.

"God, please get me home."

It was 3:47pm.

Chapter Seven

Alan entered the church and stepped down the stairs to the hall in the basement. He smelt the cooking turkey. He took in a full breath through his nose.

"So good," he said and walked into the hall. People filled the room, talking and eating with joy. A buffet lined the left wall and in rows of tables, sat the hungry Christmas crowd.

"Alan," Jim said as he approached. "I'm glad you made it. Come in and get yourself a plate. There's lots here to eat."

"Thank you so much," Alan said and smiled wide.

Alan got in line for the buffet. A few people were ahead of him. His stomach wanted him to push pass them and gorge himself, but Alan controlled himself. The line moved forward. Alan picked up a plate and peered past the people at the food. He saw dinner buns. When the line moved, he took one bun – soft and fresh – and a buttercup – cold and hard – that would be difficult to spread on the bun without tearing it. He moved along. A considerable smorgasbord lay before him.

A platter of cold cuts and cheese looked so good. He took some white cheese he thought was Havarti and a few slices of salami. Appetizing candied yams and savory brown sugar mashed turnips came next. Bowls of delicious veggies – corn, peas and carrots, and green beans in a creamy sauce enticed him. He scooped up one spoonful of each. The following dish gave him pause.

Who would bring black olives to a Christmas dinner? Horrid things.

He moved down the line before he retched.

The next dish made him say, "Uumm, stuffing." He took a deep sniff and loaded his plate. *Well-seasoned and heavenly.* After that, he came across a bunch of green stuff he could not identify. He studied it but couldn't figure out what it was. A woman walked up and filled the stuffing bowl.

"What is that?" Alan asked her and pointed at the green pile of something.

She shrugged and said, "Don't know. Someone brought it in."

Alan wanted to speak up and say, " Who brought this stuff? What is it?" But he didn't. He stared at it until the man behind him gave Alan a nudge to get moving.

"What is that?" Alan asked the man.

The man got close to it and smelled it. He appeared confused and said, "It - it's green."

Beside the green whatever it was, lay a bowl of white cheer. He knew what that was.

"Mashed potatoes," Alan said, excited. "And gravy."

He piled the potatoes over the stuffing and poured gravy over both. He stuck his finger in his gravy.

"Lumpy yet enjoyable," he said after licking it off his finger.

Alan moved on and discovered sliced, sweet honey-glazed ham ready to serve. He picked up the giant serving fork and put two slices on his plate.

"Want some?" said the fat man in a chef's uniform who stood at end of the line serving turkey.

"It's really juicy."

And inviting.

Alan held out his plate, and the chef put three pieces of breast meat on his plate.

"It looks so good," Alan said.

"Oh, it is."

Alan had piled his plate high. A table of drinks – coffee, tea, juice and eggnog – came next. Alan picked up a Styrofoam cup of red juice and turned to find a seat.

The crowded room didn't seem to yield a seat. Alan scanned to room. A tall man stood up and put his coat on, leaving an empty seat. Alan got to it in time to keep the guy behind him from getting the open seat. He sat down and put his plate and cup down.

"I'm so hungry," he said to no one in particular.

"Everyone here is," a woman said.

Alan ignored her and ate. He gulped down the mash potatoes and gravy first.

"You need to slow down and savor each bite," the same woman said.

"I can't," Alan said through the stuffing he'd stuffed into his mouth.

He ate and ate and went up for seconds. He returned to his seat and pushed ham into his mouth.

"It's like you haven't eaten in days," the woman said.

"Pretty close," he said and looked up. A redheaded beauty sat across from him. Probably five-foot-three, about 35 years old. She had a few crinkles around her eyes when she smiled at him and a grey hair or two. Awestruck, he stopped eating.

A young redhead girl, about 13 years old, sat down beside her with a plate full of desserts.

"Mom, look what I got," the girl said.

"Are you sure you got enough?" her mother said.

"Were you in church this morning?" Alan asked her.

"Yes. Were you?" the woman said.

Alan nodded. His heart pounded. Sweat burst out of his skin. He stammered and tried to say something – anything.

"I – I thought you were sisters this morning," he said.

She smiled.

"Nope," she said. "She's my daughter."

Alan decided not to say he only thought that from behind. He wanted to ask her for her name but could form the words. He fell over his tongue.

"Wha – who are –" he said and groaned.

She looked perplexed. He found her expression cute. His armpits sweated.

"What is your name, please?" Alan asked her and let out a "whew."

"Ok?" she said. "I'm Darla, and this is Chelsey."

He wanted to ask her if she was a single parent, but he said, "Where's your husband?"

Her face dropped. Her eyes glistened over with tears. He knew he had asked the wrong question. He wanted to disappear – right then.

"I'm sorry," he said.

"You have nothing to be sorry for," Darla said. "My husband died one year ago. He was killed by a drunk driver."

Chelsey started to cry.

"Oh. Sorry to hear about that."

"My daddy is not a *that*," Chelsey said with sad and angry tears on her face.

"We have to go," Darla said.

The two got up and put on their coats. They walked away. The plate of desserts went untouched. And Alan watched them leave.

Nicely done, jerk. No wonder you have such bad luck with women.

Alan pushed away his plate of seconds.

I don't deserve to eat anymore.

A woman came up to him.

"Hi. Alan?"

He glanced up and found a middle-aged woman looking down at him with eyebrows up.

"Yes." *Who is this? What's she want? Nothing good, I bet.*

"I'm Amy. I'm Jim's wife."

She stuck out her hand. Alan tried to stand up and nailed his knees into the table twice.

"Aah, ooh, ahh," he said through the pain. He rubbed his knees.

Amy put her hand over her mouth and laughed a little.

"Are you okay?" she asked.

"Yeah," Alan said, embarrassed.

He pushed his chair away from the table and stood up. He shook her hand. She motioned for him to sit back down. He did, and she sat across from him.

"May I talk to you about your situation?" she said.

"Okay."

"Jim and I run a monthly workshop that meets the first Monday of every month for people like you."

"Like me?"

"Yes. People who are struggling to make ends meet, who are unemployed or underemployed or have too much debt and are having difficulty financially. Many people want to commit suicide in these situations. We address that too. We hope you don't mind, but we discussed what you told Jim earlier. Would you like to come to the workshop?"

"That would be good, except I'm about to become homeless in the morning. I have no money and my credit cards are at their limits. And I have no job. As of tomorrow, Poof and I are on the street."

"Is that your daughter?"

"My kitty."

"Alan, we can help you. If you don't mind boarding at a church member's home, that is. There are rules though."

"What rules? I'll take anything."

"While you live there, you must be of good character. No drinking, no drugs."

"No problem there."

"Do you smoke."

"Nope."

"Good. I think we have a place for you. We have an elderly couple who will take in a boarder with a cat. Let me get a hold of them. It might be difficult today. But in the morning, I should be able to call them. When do you have to be out of your room?"

"Eleven tomorrow."

"What motel are you staying at?"

"The Sunrise. Room 18."

"I will call your room tomorrow after I talk to them. If you don't hear from me or Jim by checkout, bring your cat and your stuff and come over to the church. And we'll get you a place to stay. Sound good?"

"Yeah, it sounds real good.'

Relief waved over him. He beamed.

"Good," Amy said. "Have you had enough to eat?"

"Nope."

Alan pulled his plate back to him.

"Oh, can I take some food back for Poof? She hasn't eaten since yesterday either."

"I'll get some turkey scraps for her," Amy said.

She stood up and left the table. Alan ate some more ham – a little cold, but that was alright. Amy returned with some turkey liver, neck and a wing wrapped in foil. He thanked her and finished his plate. His stomach couldn't take anymore. He patted his gut and leaned back. He felt a belch coming on but let it out with a breath. He got up and put his coat on, stuffing the foiled turkey in his pocket.

Alan made his way to the dessert table and took some green and red tree-shaped cookies, Nanaimo bars, and some blue and white bell-shaped sugar cookies. He put the treats into his other pocket.

"As God is my witness, I'll never be hungry again," Alan said.

"*Gone With the Wind*," the woman next to him said.

And he was.

Chapter Eight

Alan arrived at his cheap motel room and entered to a loud meow. Poof hungered, and she let him know it. Alan took the foil package and opened it. The turkey meat had been removed from the bones and, along with the liver, cut into small pieces. Exactly what he needed to feed his little kitty. He spread the foil out on the floor, and Poof attacked the turkey.

He took his coat off and that's when the smell caught him.

"Phew."

He let a blast of air out his mouth.

"Someone dropped a load in here. Poof?"

He searched the room and found the poop by the bathtub with a puddle of cat pee nearby. He took some toilet paper – lots of it – and cleaned Poof's poop up.

"You stinky thing."

But he knew he couldn't blame her. He had no litter box. Last night, he wasn't expecting to find kitten, let alone be alive. He wondered what he could do. Nothing came to him. She would have to go on the floor, and he would clean it up. The Sunrise Motel people wouldn't be happy. Oh, well.

Alan sat on the bed and thought. Twenty-four hours before he wanted to die. Darkness had enveloped him. The light pierced that pitch blackness in the form of a fluffy, white and blue Ragdoll kitten. He still had a lot of darkness to deal with – crushing debt, no job, no money, no girl.

A lonely, broke life stretched out before him. Even though some help appeared, he knew a difficult journey lay ahead.

Am I up to this? he thought.

Chapter Nine

The phone rang at 10:40am, Boxing Day. He answered it.

"Hello?"

"Hi, Alan? It's Amy. We have a place for you, and you can bring Poof. Isn't that great?"

"Yes, it is. Yes, it is."

"Can you make it over to the church by noon? Do you have much stuff?"

"No, not much. A few clothes, toothbrush and Poof. Where am I going to put Poof?"

"You probably don't have a cat carrier. Do you?"

"No. Nothing.'

"What about a cardboard box you can punch holes into?"

"No. But maybe I can find one."

"Ok. See you at twelve. Bye."

Alan hung up.

"Where can I get a cardboard box? There must be one around here," he said and thought. He picked up the phone and dialed "0."

"Front desk, may I help you?" a woman said.

"This is room 18. Do you have a medium size cardboard box I can have?"

"No."

"Oh, really?"

"Wait. I know where you can get one. There's some people in room 14 who left some boxes outside their room. I think they held Christmas gifts. Hopefully, the maids haven't thrown them away yet."

"Thanks," Alan said.

He darted out the door. He looked back and forth to find room 14. He found it down the walkway, but he couldn't see any boxes. He saw a maid with her back to him, picking up a box to flatten. He needed that box before she collapsed it.

"Hey, hey. Can I have that box?" he said and raced over to her in his sock feet.

The maid appeared perplexed.

"What for?" she said.

"A box. I need a box for my cat."

"Cats aren't allowed in motel rooms."

"Don't worry, we'll be gone soon. May I have that box?"

"Okay," she said and handed it to him.

"Thank you," he said and returned to his room.

"Another cold day, Poof."

He packed his few belongings into his backpack. He poked holes into the box with a pen and put Poof into it. He closed the top by folding the flaps over.

"I better keep the top down or you'll get out.'

Poof meowed. She did not like being in there, but it had to be done. She tried to push her head through the flaps, but Alan held his hand over it. He picked up his backpack and threw it over his shoulders while holding her in the cardboard carrier. A struggle, for sure.

Alan searched the room with his eyes so he didn't forget anything and picked up the Poof box. Leaving his keycard and a messy room, Alan departed for the church. The clock read 11:53am when he closed the door. He had to get moving. He didn't want to be late and give a bad first impression.

He moved as fast as he could carrying Poof on slippery sidewalks. Across the parking lot, down the street, and toward the church, he went. Several cars were in the church parking lot. And as Alan got closer, he slipped and fell. He dropped the box, and Poof pushed her way out. She jumped out and ran away.

"Poof!"

Chapter Ten

Poof ran down the snowy pavement and turned into a driveway where Alan lost track of her.

"Poof! Come back."

Alan got up and took his backpack off. It would only slow him down, and he had to catch her. He rushed to the driveway where he lost her but couldn't find her.

"Alan," a woman called. "What's wrong?"

He turned and found Amy and two seniors – a tall man and a short woman – standing by the church entrance.

"Poof got away, and I can't find her."

"That's his cat," Amy said to the couple.

"What does she look like?" the man asked.

"She's got off-white fluffy fur with a little blue on her face. She just a kitten."

"We'll help you find her," the woman said.

The three crossed the street in a hurry.

"Which way did she go?" the man asked.

"I lost her around here somewhere."

"I'll look in backyards," the man said and started searching, peering over fences.

"I'll check under cars. We've got to find her quick," the woman said. "The longer she's gone, the harder it will be to find her."

Alan called out her name and wandered the street, searching. Amy checked bushes and around the front door steps of several homes. No luck. They went over the neighborhood. Nothing.

"Where is she?" the woman said as she bent down to look under a Chevy truck. "I think I found her. She's hiding beside a tire under this truck." She pointed at the cat.

With care and stealth, they surrounded the vehicle. Each one bent down and peeked under.

"She's going to run as soon as we try to grab her," the woman said. "Tom, I will call to her to get her attention, and you grab her from behind."

Tom nodded and settled behind the tire.

"I'm ready, Grace."

"Psst, psst," Grace said.

Poof watched her but didn't move. Tom reached around the tire, but she darted off out into the street as an SUV sped toward her. Poof stopped in the road.

"Oh no," Grace said.

"Poof!"

The driver hit the breaks, but the slippery roads and the momentum of the vehicle caused it to run over Poof. Grace turned away.

"Please, God," Alan said.

Poof lay crouched in the street as the SUV came to a stop. She didn't move. Alan ran up to her and got down on his knees.

"Poof?"

Grace, Tom and Amy came to them.

"Is she okay?" Amy asked.

"Poof?"

And the little cat stood up.

Alan picked her up and looked her over. No blood and she didn't cry out in pain as if she'd been injured.

"I think she's alright," Alan said.

"Thank God," Tom said.

"The SUV must have ran over top of her with out hitting her. What luck," Amy said.

"Thank you, God. Thank you, Jesus," Alan said and hugged Poof.

Tom and Grace retrieved Alan's backpack and the box. Alan placed his kitten back inside the makeshift carrier. He held it shut with two hands, top and bottom. He did not want her getting out again.

"Thank you for your help," he said. "I just got her. She saved my life."

"And you saved hers at the same time," Amy said.

"I gotta hear that story," Tom said.

"But right now, we'll get you to your new home. It's lunch time," Grace said.

"I'm Alan."

Tom and Grace introduced themselves. They got Alan and Poof into their Nitro. Alan thanked Amy, and they left. They arrived at Alan's new, temporary home. An average house in a nice neighborhood. After getting inside, they showed Alan his new room. He unpacked his few belongings and let Poof out of the box. She started to explore the bedroom. He watched her.

"Are we in a new place, Poof?"

He sat on the bed, not knowing what to do. He felt lucky and thanked God. Someone knocked on the door. Grace came in and put her hands on her hips.

"You don't have to stay in here. I have someone I want you to meet. Leave Poof here."

Alan followed her out of his room, closing the door behind him and locking Poof in. They went to the living room where Alan saw an orange tabby.

"This is Rex. We got him from the SPCA, oh about a year and a half ago."

"Aww," Alan said. "He reminds me of Buster. He's an orange one too. I left him behind when I moved out here. I miss him."

Alan bent down and got closer to Rex. The cat stretched his neck out to sniff Alan's fingers that reached toward him. He smelled Alan. Rex allowed Alan to scratch him about the head and neck. Alan laughed when Rex pushed his head into Alan's hand.

"Yeah, he's a friendly fellow. Quite the suck. We'll have to gradually introduce Rex to Poof to cut down on the hissing, growling and swatting," Grace said.

"For sure," Alan said.

He wondered where Kim was. He had to get his life together and find a better woman.

Good luck with that. Kim was the best I ever found. And I'm better off without her.

Chapter Eleven

Eight days after moving in with Tom and Grace, Alan had no success in finding a job. Because the Christmas holidays were over, employers weren't looking to hire. Fast food work was a possibility but only as a last resort.

Alan spent his mornings applying for positions and afternoons helping around the house, cleaning, making repairs, shoveling snow or anything else that he could do. Evenings, he watched television and watched Rex and Poof. He tolerated her attacks, and she played with him.

Early in the new year, a knock at the front door got Alan's attention. Grace answered it. Alan stopped playing with Poof and went to see who was there.

"Hi, Sweetheart," Grace said. "Come in."

Grace moved out of the way, and Darla entered. Alan recognized her as the redheaded woman he had met at the church dinner. The one he had put his foot in his mouth in front of. He smiled, wide.

"Alan, this is my daughter, Darla."

"Hi Darla. I-I'm Alan."

"We met at the Christmas dinner, Mom."

"Really? Let's go into the kitchen," Grace said. "Coffee?"

"Love some," Darla said.

"Me too," Alan said.

They went into the kitchen and Grace turned on the coffee maker.

"Alan's having some trouble finding a new job," Grace said as they sat at the table. "He's got nothing but his cat, and he has to work. Do you think there's anything open at the Co-op?"

"Maybe," Darla said.

"Darla's a cashier at the grocery store, so she might be able to help you get a position."

"I can't get him a job in the same department. But I heard a food clerk is leaving to work in the oil patch. So he could apply for that position."

"How does that sound?" Grace asked.

"Great," Alan said. "You'll put a good word in for me?"

"Yep," Darla said.

"Thank you. Thank you."

He wanted to thank her for being so cute but not now, if ever. Grace served them some coffee.

"Where are you from?" Darla asked.

"Oshawa."

"Ontario?"

"Yes."

"How did you end up here? In the Falls?"

"My ex" - he emphasized "ex" – "girlfriend wanted to move here. But I miss Oshawa."

"Where is she now?" Grace asked.

"I don't know. She threw me out, and I haven't seen her since."

Alan looked down at his coffee.

"Oh," Darla said.

"Maybe he doesn't want to talk about it, Sweetheart."

"Sorry," Darla said and touched his arm.

She turned to her mother and changed the subject to her day at work. Grace and Darla talked, and he felt left out. He'd blown it with her and he knew it.

They heard a soft mew.

"Who is that? Is that your cat, Alan? I know Rex's meow. That's not Rex," Darla said.

"That's Poof," Alan said.

They looked under the table and found her.

"You can tell a cat by his meow?" Alan asked. "Rex isn't even your cat."

"I've heard Rex's meows enough to know when it's not him."

Alan reached down and picked up Poof. He stood up, holding her.

"Aww, she's beautiful. Poof isn't it?" Darla said.

"Yes," Alan said and scratched his kitten between the ears, and she purred.

"Where did you get her?" Darla asked.

"She saved my life."

"Oh, I gotta hear this."

Alan sat back down and told his story of Christmas Eve in the cold and finding a lost kitty. He watched her watching him as he spoke, her eyes wide and bright.

"That's amazing," she said when he finished. "Good thing you two found each other."

With a smile, she reached out and touched his arm, leaving her hand there.

"We've got a cat too," she said.

"Rex? He's cute. I love orange ones."

"No, silly. Our cat. Well, my daughter's cat. She got him for Christmas last year. Do you like Tuxedo cats?"

"Tuxedo?"

"Yes," she said. "They're black and white cats that look like they have a tuxedo on. Some people call them 'Tuxies'."

"I never thought – I just thought they were black and white cats. Neat."

"What's his name?"

"Capone."

"Where did you get him?"

The two women glanced at each other.

"SPCA," Grace said.

She reached out and held Darla's hand. Had he asked the wrong question again?

"It's okay, Mom," Darla said. "My husband was killed by a drunk driver, bringing Capone home for my daughter's Christmas present."

"I'm sorry," Alan said.

"It happened over a year ago on Christmas Eve," Grace said.

Silence.

"I'm managing," Darla said.

Alan felt the heel.

"I'm going to go," Darla said. "Chelsey will be getting home from school soon."

"Okay, Honey."

They stood up, and Darla went to the front door.

"Alan, I'll see you again. I'll tell Human Resources you'll be coming in. Tomorrow would be a good idea. Bye. I love Poof."

Grace and Darla said," Good-bye." They hugged and Darla walked out the door.

*

And she saw him again. She helped him land the job at the Co-op Grocery Store. Her visits to Grace and Tom's home became more frequent, and she always included him in her visits. Alan called on her at home, and they went for walks, movies, and Langston Falls Lions hockey games. And they talked.

Many times the topic of conversation centred on cats – Poof, Capone, an Orange Tabby Darla had named Red, a Siamese called Tia from Alan's childhood, and Buster.

One evening, Alan leaned over and kissed her lips. She kissed back.

In the spring, Alan found an apartment and moved out of Tom and Grace's home. He thanked them with all his heart. Without them, he would be homeless and loveless and probably dead.

He spent much of his free time at Darla's home. They enjoyed each other's company with more conversation, playing games with Chelsey and watch television. Alan got to know Darla and Chelsey, and they got to know him. Whenever Alan met up with Darla, he felt special. She warmed and excited him. He had found the right woman. Each morning, he couldn't wait to be with her at work and more so afterwards.

In October, he asked her to marry him.

She said," Yes!"

They celebrated and spread the good news. Announcements went in *The Langston Falls News* and on their Facebook profiles. And they told everybody they knew or saw. The future looked bright for the glowing couple, but a darkness would soon re-enter Alan's life.

*

"Welcome to The Second Chance Workshop again. How is everybody?" Jim said.

Several men said they were fine, the rest stayed quiet. Alan nodded and smiled. Alan had had his second chance and was back on his feet. He had a good job and had gotten engaged. He didn't need the workshop anymore, but Jim asked him to come this Monday evening and share his success story. They sat in a circle of chairs. Eleven men and two women attended along with Jim and Alan.

"We have a special guest tonight. Alan will be telling his story. But first, I want to share something," Jim said.

"Last week, the police were called to the Maple Avenue Bridge as a man sat on the ledge, ready to jump into the freezing waters below. The police talked to him and tried to convince him that whatever was bothering him it wasn't worth his life. The man kept saying he had lost everything and that it was hopeless. The police tried to distract him and pull him to safety. But this man who had lost hope jumped to his death. He'd given up. Whereas, you – all of you – have felt the same way. But you haven't taken your own lives. Some of you have come close, but thanks to Jesus, you are still here. You are stronger than the man on the bridge. You've all been through hell and felt hopeless. With God, there is always hope. With hope there is strength. Don't be like the man on the bridge. I will be conducting his funeral Thursday. You are stronger than him.

"Now, let me introduce you to Alan. He went through that hopelessness too. He wanted to die, tried to commit suicide. And he's here to tell his story. Alan."

Alan spoke his story of how Kim ruined him, how foolish he felt, blamed himself and lost hope. But he found something – his Ragdoll kitten – that gave him purpose and a reason to live. He

101

pulled himself out of his despair with the help of Jim and Amy, Grace and Tom, and the Lord. He secured a new job and will get married next year. All because he found a reason to live – Poof.

"Thanks, Alan," Jim said. "When you are feeling like taking that last step, find something to give you reason to live. It can be anything your mother or father, a child, a son, a daughter, a dog or even a small kitten. And, of course, Christ. Tough times don't last, tough people do. Remain strong and the rest shall pass. Any questions?"

"Alan, how did you take care of all your debt?" one man asked.

"I declared bankruptcy. It was difficult, but I had no choice. A light in the tunnel came when they repossessed Kim's car. When I heard, it made my day. I'll tell ya."

"What would you do if she wanted to get back together with you?" another one said.

"Hit the road, you..."Alan said without finishing his sentence.

"It would be pretty hard for her to hit the road without a car," one of them said.

"I'd give her my beater. So long as she left," Alan said and got a laugh.

The meeting ended. Alan drove home in his debt free 1996 Dodge Caravan with the bent bumper he'd bought a few weeks before. As he drove, he thought about his good fortune. And Kim, too.

Chapter Twelve

Alan and Darla sat on her couch watching Netflix, and when *Heaven Is For Real* rolled the final credits, Alan turned to his wife-to-be.

"I want to move back to Oshawa after we get married," he said.

"Wait. What? Really?" Darla said.

"Well, my mom's there. I have my friends there. And I don't like it here."

"I'm here. Isn't that enough?"

"I have no friends here."

"What are you talking about? You have friends here."

"It's not the same. I miss home."

"And I'll miss my home, my parents and my friends if we move down east. Did you think about that?"

"We'll come to visit every few years."

"Every few years? Are you serious? I don't want to leave Langston Falls behind. I want to stay here. Besides, do you know what it's like to sell a house in a depressed market and move everything thousands of miles away? It's expensive. And what about Chelsey? She'll leave all her friends behind. It's tough for 12-year-old girls to make new friends in a new school. Girls are cliquey at that age. It will cost too much."

"Money, eh? That's what you're really thinking of? I already had a woman that only cared about money. You're just another one."

"Another one what?"

"Another Kim."

"I am not 'another Kim.' How dare you? Since when have I ever taken money from you?"

"You will. I can tell. I can see it now. She didn't take my money at first –"

"I am not Kim! Don't you dare say I'm her. I am not."

"You will. I know you will," he said.

"Alright, get out."

"What?"

"Get out! I want you out."

"You don't want me here?"

"No. Out."

She stood up and pointed at the door.

He sat and stared at her, aghast.

"I'm pointing at the door. Don't you get it? Out."

"Oh, I get it," he said. "I'm gone."

He got up and left with a slam of the door. She opened the door and said, "Good."

And she slammed the door.

"Good riddance."

Chapter Thirteen

Alan arrived at his apartment, went in and slammed the door. Poof laid on the back of the couch and ran under the kitchen table from the noise.

"Who does she think she is?"

He wanted to yell and call her names he would never repeat in church company. But he didn't. Instead, he paced around his old apartment and muttered. This went on for half an hour until he sighed and sat down. Poof joined him, stretching out on his lap upside down. He laughed at her.

"Are we broken up now? Should I call her, Poof? No. She should call me."

The door buzzer sounded. Alan put Poof aside and went to the security panel.

Is that her?

"Hello?" he said when he pushed the talk button.

"Hello? Alan?"

A woman's voice?

He could barely hear her through the defective speaker.

"I'm sorry," she said. "Can I come up?"

Alan pushed door release button to let her in. He waited by the door until he heard a knock. He opened the door and found Kim standing there.

"Kim? What are you doing here?"

"I missed you," she said.

She stepped in close to him. He didn't back away.

"How did you find me?"

"Facebook."

"What are you doing here?"

"I missed you, my man."

She ran her hand up his arm, like she had before.

"You think I'd take you back after what you and that guy did to me?"

"He made me do it."

"Really? You want me to believe that?"

He wanted to believe her.

"I never wanted to do it, but he would hit me and said he'd kill me if I didn't do it. I'm so sorry."

She looked up at him with pleading, sorrowful eyes.

"How do I know he didn't send you here?"

"He's gone. I kicked him out. He took all my money so I finally sent him away."

"Where is he now?"

She shrugged.

"I'm just glad he's gone. It'll never happen again. I swear. I only want us to be together again."

Poof came to the door and brushed her leg. She looked down, disgusted.

"You have another cat?"

Alan picked up Poof and scratched her.

"She stays with me," he said.

Her face changed to a forced smile.

"I can get used to a cat. What his name?"

"Her name is Poof."

"She's cute."

Kim moved up for a kiss, and Alan kissed her. She took his hand and led him to the bedroom. Alan hadn't made love to Darla. They had decided to wait until their honeymoon. But he didn't want to wait with Kim. When they finished, she cuddled into him.

"So, are we back together again?" she asked him.

He nodded. And thought about Darla.

Chapter Fourteen

Several days past, and Alan's mind turned to Darla. Kim had moved in with him.

Did I make a mistake? he thought.

Alan showed up an Darla's doorstep. He rang. She answered.

"Hi," he said.

"Hi."

"Are you okay?"

"Fine."

Tension.

"I've gotten back together with Kim."

"What?!"

Tears filled her angry blue eyes.

"Well, you split up with me."

"I didn't break up with you. We had a fight. And you ran back to her? After what she did?"

"She's different now."

"No, she's not. People like her don't change."

"Why did you throw me out?"

Capone came to the open door and tried to get out. Alan lifted him up.

"Come in. I don't want Capone getting out."

Alan brought the Tuxedo Cat in and closed the door.

"How's Poof?" she said.

"She's okay."

"Remember, she hates cats. She made you get rid of Buster. She'll do that with Poof."

"She's changed."

"No, she hasn't."

"How can you say that? You don't know her?"

"Before I met Ken, I went out with a guy like her. He treated me like dirt and stole money from me. I would break up with him, and he'd come back and apologize. He'd tell me he'd never do it again. But after a few weeks, he'd be back to his jerkwater ways. She's already proven to you what she's like. She will go back to her old ways. They always do."

"I don't know," Alan said.

He reached out and took her hand.

"I don't know what to do. And she's here now."

"You have to decide," she said.

"I can't decide between the two of you."

She ripped her hand out of his.

"If you can't decide, I'll decide for you. Get out. And don't come back."

"Darla."

"Get out. We're over. So over."

Alan turned and opened the door. He looked back at her, knowing he'd done wrong. He'd maltreated a good woman. And he didn't know what to do about it. Kim waited at home. He sat in his van, deciding. And he left, knowing he'd never come back.

Chapter Fifteen

Alan drove, meandering his route home. He went inside. He got Poof, held her and cried, burying his face in her deep, soft fur. She stayed still, and his tears wet her. She purred and got scratched.

"How a cat can make someone feel better," he said. "Is she holding Capone right now?"

After a while, Kim came in carrying shopping bags from several different stores.

"You went shopping?" Alan said.

"Yeah," she said, drawing the word out in sarcasm.

"Where did you get the money? I thought Bill took all your money?"

She hesitated.

"I had some hidden in a savings account."

He knew she lied. He had ruined it with Darla and had gotten back together with a liar. Yet, Kim kept him from being alone. He hated to be alone. A rotten woman is better than no woman. At least, he had Poof.

Chapter Sixteen

Alan stopped going to church so he wouldn't see her. Besides, Kim didn't like it. He avoided her at work, but sometimes he had to be near her. At times, she would say, "Hi" other times not. Did she maybe want to see him again? He didn't know. He sat down one day and wrote:

I don't know if I will ever hold her again
I don't know if I will brush away her tears when life hurts
I don't know if I can work by her side without being by her
side
I don't know where this is going or how to get there

She makes love without touching me
She smiles and I am glad
With her I am immortalized
With her I can fly

Did my chance fade away?
Did my love find another?
Can I find another way?
Can I help but wonder?

I wasn't looking to love

I was looking to live
I don't know
God, I don't know

Take this uncertainty away
There has to be a way
But I am lost
And I have paid the price

I tore her heart out
And she ripped herself from me
What can I do to repair the damage?
I don't know how to fix us

I ask, what have I done to deserve this?
And yet, I already know the answer
Can she forgive me?
That I don't know

He wanted to give the poem to her but couldn't.
She probably doesn't want to see it anyhow.

Alan rested back into his recliner and put his poem on the end table. He sighed. He felt tears coming on when Poof leaped onto his lap and walked up and down on him until she settled on the chair's arm. Alan laid his hand on his leg.

Poof bent down and rubbed her face and head into his hand, back and forth, over and over. She purred. Alan's tears failed to develop. Alan's heavy heart lightened.

Poof stopped rubbing and began rolling around Alan's lap and the chair. She rolled so much she fell to the floor. She tried to break her fall by clawing into the chair and pulling herself up, but she hit the floor. Alan giggled.

"You're quite the Poof, Poofer."

She jumped back up and curled up on his lap. He petted her.

"I love you, Poof. My gift from God."

*

One Saturday, Alan and Poof spent the evening watching television when the door buzzed. Alan answered it and let Pastor Jim in.

"I'm surprised to see you," Alan said.

He hadn't seen Jim in months.

"I was concerned about you," Jim said. "May I come in?"

"Yes, yes. Would you like a Coke? Coffee?"

"A Coke would be nice."

Alan got him a can from the fridge and one for himself. He turned off the t.v. They sat at the kitchen table.

"How have you been, Alan?"

"Uuh, okay."

"Where's your girlfriend?"

"I don't know. She's out. Sometimes she goes out. I don't know where she goes. She won't tell me. She comes home late at night stinking of alcohol and her hair and clothes a mess."

Poof came into the kitchen and rubbed Jim's leg. He looked down.

:Well, look who's gotten bigger," Jim said.

"Yeah, she's no longer a kitten. Just a big ball 'o fur. My Poofer."

"And what's your girlfriend's name again?"

"Kim."

"And Kim doesn't have a problem with Poof?"

"Yes, she does. She'll come into bed on the few nights she stays home and if Poof is on the bed, she'll throw her out of the room. 'No cats on the bed,' she'll say. Poof is scared of her. I think she hits Poof, but I haven't seen it. She keeps accusing me of loving Poof more than her."

"Do you?"

"Yep," Alan said.

He ran his fingers down her back, and she pushed her bum in the air.

"How are you money wise?"

"Okay."

"Has she taken money from you?"

"She borrows money every week."

"Does she pay it back?"

"Uhh, no."

113

"Is she working?"

"Nope."

"So you're financing her nightlife?"

"Pretty much, I guess."

"What happened to Kim's ex-boyfriend?"

"She said she split up with him because he stole all her money. That he made her steal my money and basically ruin me. Why?"

"Was his name Bill?"

"Yeah. How did you know that?"

"Remember the suicide we discussed in the workshop? The man who threw himself off the Maple Avenue Bridge?"

"Yes."

"His name was Bill Standnik. He left a suicide note that his family shared with me. He said his girlfriend ruined him. She convinced him to get credit cards, a line of credit, and a car loan in his name. She left him $56,000.00 in debt. A debt he couldn't pay off. He decided suicide was his only way out. He named her in the note: Kimberly."

Alan's mouth dropped open.

"That's no coincidence," Alan said.

"No, I don't think so either."

"That – that—"

Alan wanted to curse and swear but didn't because a man of God sat across from him.

"I can't believe she did that," Alan said. "She asked me to get her a credit card, but because of my bankruptcy, I don't have a good credit rating. So no credit cards. Thank God. I bet she's doing it to whoever she goes out and sees when she's gone for hours. I bet she's doing it right now."

"What are you going to do about it?"

"I don't know. I really blew it with Darla. Does she still go to church?"

"Yes, she does. She asked me to come and see you. To see how you're doing. She's concerned you might try to hurt yourself."

"I'm stronger than that now. Is she seeing anyone now?"

"I think she's gone on a few coffee dates but nothing serious."

Alan felt a pang of jealousy then relief.

"I should call her," Alan said.

"Will you come back to church? That would make a big difference."

"Yes, I will."

"Good. I look forward to seeing you there. It's getting late, and I've got an early service in the morning that I still have to prepare for. See you there."

They shook hands, and Jim left.

Alan paced the living room and thought about what he would say to Kim. As the night wore on, he looked forward to it more and more. It was 11:10pm.

Chapter Seventeen

At 1:30am, Alan heard Kim try to slide her key into the lock. She failed.

Too drunk.

Alan unlocked and yanked the door open. He glared at her. She stumbled in and reeked of liquor with her clothes disheveled.

"What happened to Bill?" he asked her.

"Bill who? I don't know."

"I'll tell you. He killed himself because of you. You broke him just like you did to me."

"I didn't 'break' anyone," Kim said and swore.

"You broke me. I almost commit suicide because of what you did. Bill didn't make you charge up my credit cards and steal my money. You did it yourself."

"Yeah, so. You know, you're lucky to have me. You can't do any better than me. You're short...fat...ugly. A loser."

"I'm a loser? The only way you get by is by stealing from guys you make fall in love with you. Using your looks and sex to manipulate them."

"At least, I have looks. Not like your 'fiancé.' Oh, wait. She's no longer your fiancé."

"Darla is beautiful."

"Ugly redhead with too many freckles."

"She loved me. Me. 'A loser'."

"Where is she now? Not here. I'm here. Right now."

"I'd rather live here alone with Poof than spend one more minute with you."

"I hate that cat. I hate all cats."

"Darla loves Poof. I never should've gotten back together with you. I don't deserve you. You're filth. I cannot love a woman like you, especially if she hates cats."

"Sshhh," she said. "Calm down, lover. We can go back to Oshawa. That's what you want, isn't it? She won't go there. And you can keep Poof."

"I'd stay if I could get her back. Besides, you're messing around with some guy or guys. I don't know. You'll do the same thing to him. You'll ruin him too. We've over. I want you out. Right now."

"I will destroy you."

"You already have."

"No one breaks up with me."

Kim pushed past Alan and staggered into the living room. He followed. Poof lay curled up on the recliner, and she picked her up.

"What are you doing?" Alan asked.

"Destroying you. You love this cat more than me.'

Kim threw Poof across the room. She slammed in an end table and struck the wall. She yowled and dropped to the floor without landing on her feet.

"Poof!"

Alan screamed and ran to his precious Ragdoll Cat. She lay twisted on the carpet, not moving. He kneeled beside her.

"That felt so good," Kim said.

"Get out! Get out before I tear you in half."

Kim ran for the door and got out with her life and nothing more.

Poof breathed but otherwise did not move. Alan took out his iPhone out of his pocket and dialed her veterinarian's emergency number.

"Come on, come on," he said as it rang.

A woman answered.

"Cypress Hills Veterinarian Clinic. Is this an emergency?"

"Yes. My girlfriend threw my cat and now she's not moving. I have to get her in. Now."

"Is she breathing?"

"Yes."

"Is she bleeding?"

"No."

"What is your name?"

"Alan Barton. Can I bring her in now? It has to be now."

"Yes. I will contact the vet on call. She will meet you at the clinic. Alan, you need to carefully move your cat. She may have internal injuries. Do you have something flat to slide her onto? Like a wood panel or a baking sheet?"

"I have a baking sheet."

"Good. Get it and slowly, carefully slide it beneath her," the operator said.

Alan put the phone down, got the baking sheet and pushed it under Poof with utmost care. Alan picked up his cell.

"I got her," he said.

"Now bring – what's your cat's name?"

"Her name is Poof."

"Bring her in. The vet is on her way. You going to be okay?"

"I've got her. I think so."

"Do you want me to stay on the phone with you?"

"No. I need to put my phone down to carry her."

"Good luck, Alan.'

He hung up and replaced his cell in his pocket. Gently, he picked up the baking sheet, and as quickly as he could without moving her, he took her out to his van. After opening the passenger door, he placed her on the front seat and got on his way to the animal clinic.

"Poof, please be okay. Please be okay," he said all the way there.

Normally a ten-minute drive, Alan got there in five. The longest ride of his life.

Chapter Eighteen

When Alan arrived at the pet hospital, the lights were off. He had got there before the doctor. He pulled into the parking lot, parked and turned off the ignition. He looked down at Poof. She had not moved. But she breathed.

She's still alive. A good sign. Where's that vet?

He lowered his head, closed his eyes and clasped his hands together.

"Lord Jesus, please help her. Please let her be okay. I'll do anything, just make sure Poof is okay."

He lifted his head and opened his eyes. A light shone inside the clinic. A woman unlocked the front door. Alan got out of the van and rushed to the door. He threw the door open and called out.

"I'm the guy who called. Are you the vet?"

"Yes," the woman said. "I'm Doctor Westly. Where's your cat?"

"In the van. I didn't want to move her. She's hurt bad."

"Let's go get her."

They exited the building and got to the van. Alan opened the passenger door and the doctor leaned in. With care, she picked up the baking sheet. She took Poof into the hospital and into an examination room. He followed.

"She's breathing," Doctor Westly said.

She examined Poof, running her hands over her, feeling along her back. She took out her stethoscope and listened to Poof. She looked inside her mouth and ears.

"I have to do some x-rays," she said. "You can wait in the reception area."

Dr. Westly took Poof out of the exam room and down the hallway. Alan sat in the waiting area. His heart pounded hard and he trembled a little. He prayed again. And he called Darla.

He told her what happened, and she said she'd be right there. Fifteen minutes later, she joined Alan in the waiting room. He went to her, and they wrapped their arms around each other. He sobbed.

"She'll be okay. You'll see," Darla said.

Alan nodded. They parted after a few minutes and sat down. She took his hand.

"Why would she do that?" Alan asked.

"She's not a good person," Darla said.

Doctor Westly emerged from the back.

"Alan, it's not good news."

Darla gasped, and Alan squeezed her hand.

"Her spinal cord is severed. I'm amazed she's still breathing. There's nothing I can do."

Alan cried, and Darla held him.

"I know this is difficult. But I need your permission to put her down. She will only suffer if we don't."

"Oh, God," Alan said. "I don't want her hurting anymore. You can do it. She's such a good kitty. Such a wonderful cat. She saved my life, but now I can't save her's."

Tears streamed down their faces.

"What would you like me to do with the remains?" the vet asked.

"I don't know. She was so happy with me."

"Would you like us to dispose of the remains?"

"Yes."

"I'm sorry," Dr. Westly said.

Alan and Darla got up and left the building into the darkness of the night.

Chapter Nineteen

Each in their own vehicles, Alan and Darla drove to her place. Alan's eyes teared up, making his vision blurry. He took it slow on the icy roads. They got there and went inside. Capone met them at the door and meowed, demanding to get fed. He ran to his food dish in the kitchen, and they came with him.

"You hungry?" Darla said to the noisy kitty.

She fed him. Alan reached down and scratched him. More tears came on, but he held them in. Capone ate like he hadn't eaten in days. By the look of him, he's been fed everyday all day.

Darla hugged Alan and led him to the living room couch. They sat side-by-side, saying nothing. What could be said?

After some time, she said, "How are you?"

He shrugged. He wanted to cry but didn't.

"She was such a good kitty," he said after a long pause. "She would always sleep in the strangest positions. I brought home a cardboard box, and she sat and lied in it for hours. Why would a cat want to just sit in a box?"

"Yeah, no kidding. Capone does the same thing. Crazy cats," she said with a little laugh.

Alan gazed into her eyes. Tears developed, but this time they were not for Poof.

"I'm sorry," he said.

"For what?"

"For letting that – that witch back in my life and for hurting you. She's nothing but trouble. You – you – you're the best thing that's ever happened to me."

Darla's own tears appeared.

"With Poof a close second," he said.

Darla laughed.

"She had such beautiful blue eyes. Powder blue eyes."

"So do you."

He kissed her.

"I love you."

"Me too," she said. "I was so worried about you with her. She almost got you to end it all. I thought she might do it again."

"I wouldn't do it again. Poof showed me there's a lot to live for. Like you. Without her, I would have never met you."

"Without her, you'd be dead."

"Without the Lord, I'd be dead. It's going to be one year since he sent her to me tomorrow."

"Do you still want to go back to Oshawa?"

She rubbed his hand.

"No. Not if it means I have to leave you. I can't leave you."

"What about your friends, your family, and your mom?"

"I miss them, but I want to stay here with you."

Darla wrapped her arms around her man and held him close. They basked in their love for each other. But Capone broke it up. He jumped onto Darla's lap and put his paw on her shoulder. She turned to her daughter's cat.

"What, Capone? I think someone's jealous," she said.

Alan petted him, and he got down. The couple spent the evening being with each other. A warmness made them glow. He wanted to make love to her, but decided to wait for their honeymoon. They fell asleep holding each other.

*

Their honeymoon came the following summer. Pastor Jim performed their wedding service. Alan's mother came across the country to attend, and Chelsey welcomed her new father.

124

Soon, Darla became pregnant and then a little boy came along. Alan had a time he never dreamed could be. He never forgot Poof – the reason he now had this wonderful life.

As for Kim, Alan turned to his wife and said, "You made me forget about her. Thank you."

Jasper: A Siamese Story

Chapter One

"Grandma, I need a favor," Sharon said to her only living relative.

"What is it, honey?"

"My cancer surgery has been booked for Tuesday in Calgary. Will you take care of Jasper for me?"

"I can't," Vera said into her phone.

"Grandma, I've tried everybody else."

"What about a kennel?"

"I can't afford a kennel. With the surgery and chemotherapy, I could be out of work for months. And I only have so much in savings."

"I don't know, not at my age."

"He's easy to take care of."

"I've never had a cat before. I like dogs. Not cats."

"You can like cats too."

"No, I can't."

"It's only temporary, Grandma."

"I don't know."

"All you do is feed him, make sure his water dish is full and clean out his litter box once a day."

"What if he gets sick?"

"Then you'll have to take him to the vet."

"No, I can't. The SPCA will watch him. Try them."

"No. They'll give him away. Or worse. Please, Grandma."

"I-I'm not sure."

"Grandma, I need you now. I only have you and Jasper. Please, Grandma. I really need you."

"I guess so."

"Thank you. Thank You! It's only for a little while. I'll be over this cancer in no time. Can I bring him over tomorrow afternoon?"

"I suppose."

"See you then. Thanks, Grandma. I'll bring everything you'll need. He's easy to care for, you'll see."

"Alright. Tomorrow then. Bye."

Click.

"What am I going to do with a cat?"

Chapter Two

The next day after lunch, Sharon arrived at her grandmother's home in northeast Langston Falls. After a knock, Vera let her in.

Sharon carried in a cat carrier and a reusable shopping bag and set them on the floor. The young Siamese meowed a few times. Sharon hugged her grandmother - a warm embrace on a cold day.

"This is Jasper," Sharon said and picked up the carrier. Jasper continued meowing.

"He makes a lot of noise. I heard Siamese cats have a loud meow. I like it quiet."

"He usually only meows when he's hungry. Otherwise, he's not too talkative, and this is a new place for him."

Vera's brow crossed.

I don't want to impose on her, but I've got no choice. I don't want to lose Jasper, my furry baby boy.

"I brought a bag of Whiskas, some Temptations treats, cat litter, his litter box and dishes. We should set his stuff up before we let him out to explore."

Sharon picked up the green bag, and they put everything in its place - water in a dish, litter in the box and food in the cupboard.

"When should I feed him?"

"In the morning when you get up and before you go to bed. Give him a quarter cup each time. He'll remind you when it's dinnertime. Trust me, he'll remind you."

Vera rolled her eyes. They went back to the talkative Siamese, and Sharon let him out. Jasper stepped out of the cat cage. His eyes wide, he looked from side-to-side and meowed. He sniffed around his new surroundings - first the living room and onto the kitchen.

"You want some tea?"

"Love some."

After the water boiled and tea bags were dipped and squeezed, they sat down in the living room.

"I'm worried, honey. Your mother died of breast cancer. And I'm afraid you will too."

Sharon reached over and held her hand.

"The doctor said they caught it early. They're going to do some minor surgery to remove the small lump and then I have some chemotherapy to go through to make sure the cancer is gone. They've come a long way in treating breast cancer since Mom died twenty years ago."

"She had it early, like you. She was only 28 when she died. By the time she went in for treatment, it was too late."

"I know you're worried. But I'll be fine. Oh, before I forget, you have to make sure Jasper's food is put away or he'll get into it."

Jasper walked down the hall toward the bedrooms.

"He's such a cute kitty, Grandma. He loves to play with a string or just about anything he can bat around."

Jasper returned to the living room and announced his presence.

"I'm gonna miss him," Sharon said with tears in her eyes. "Grandma, I'm scared."

Vera put her arms around her granddaughter and pulled her close.

"You're young and strong, honey. You'll make it through. They caught it early. Jasper will be here when you're ready to take him back. I'll take care of him. You can do it."

Sharon nodded, and they pulled apart. Sharon wiped her tears.

"I have to go. My surgery is tomorrow morning but I have to be there tonight. And it's a long drive."

"Okay, honey."

They stood up, and Sharon picked up Jasper. She hugged and kissed him, and he purred.

"I want to hold you forever."

She put him down after some more loves. He sat beside her with his head up. Sharon held back the tears, hugged Vera and said, "Good-bye."

And she was gone.

*

Vera waved and her granddaughter drove away. She closed the door and wept. She took out a Kleenex, dabbed her eyes, then returned to the couch. She drew in heavy breaths and sobbed. She hadn't cried like that since James died.

A softness touched her arm. Jasper put his paws on her. He moved up toward her head and pushed his face into hers. Vera pulled away, still Jasper nudged her cheek. She stopped crying and ran her fingers through his fur. Her eyes smiled. She petted him down his brown back.

"No wonder she loves you."

Chapter Three

At 7:50am the next morning, Vera woke to Jasper curled beside her. She scratched him between his ears. She got out of bed, went for a pee and washed. Time to feed Jasper and herself.

Why isn't he meowing for food? she thought. *Like Sharon said he would. I fed him last night so he should be hungry. I hope nothing's wrong.*

Vera went back to her bedroom. Jasper still lay on her comforter.

"It seems you're not hungry this morning."

She stepped into the kitchen where cat food covered the floor. She forgot to put the bag of cat food in the cupboard, and he tore a large hole in it. Not only had he gorged himself, he played with the food and made an awful mess. Whiskas everywhere.

"Why you little...bad cat. Bad, bad cat."

Vera retrieved the broom and dustpan from the kitchen closet and swept up the hard cat food, dumping it back into the bag with some falling out the hole.

"What am I going to do with this bag, Jasper?"

From the cupboard above the refrigerator, she took out a sizable plastic container with a snap-on lid that she used to keep oatmeal in.

"Perfect."

Vera poured the cat food into the container with some spilling onto the floor. She cleaned up the rest of the it and snapped the lid shut. The container went into the cupboard.

"Let's see you rip that open, bad cat. Bad Jasper. Sharon better get better soon. Otherwise, I don't know what I'm going to do with you...you...you naughty kitty."

Chapter Four

Six months before her breast cancer diagnosis, Sharon answered an online ad from someone giving away kittens.

It would be great to have a cat again. Since jerkwad made me get rid of Bubbles. I miss her. But not him. I'm so glad he moved out.

She got the address and drove over that evening. A woman greeted her at the door and took her inside to the kittens. The mother, a Siamese, had five kitties - three were Siamese, one an Oriental Shorthair, and a Siamese/Tabby mix.

"We tried to keep her indoors when she went into heat, but the horny little Manx got out and had a field day. She obviously mated with more than one Tom. The neighbors have a Siamese male who's not fixed so we figure he got to her along with some of his friends," the woman said.

"I like the Siamese ones."

She picked up one that pushed away from her. She put that one down and got another - a boy. He cuddled into Sharon and purred.

"That's Jasper".

"How old is he?"

"Eight weeks or so."

Sharon kissed Jasper and held him close.

"He doesn't seem to mind being kissed."

"Yeah, he's a suck."

"I'll take him." Sharon rubbed her face into his.

*

The first night with her, Jasper searched his new surroundings. He settled into Sharon and her apartment and the routine of being fed twice a day with some occasional treats.

One evening after Sharon had gone to bed, Jasper invaded the garbage can and ate some left over Kraft Dinner. Sharon awoke to garbage littering the kitchen.

"You stink. You'll eat anything."

Sharon removed the plants from her home to prevent Jasper from eating them and being poisoned. She put away all the human food after meals or he would steal it and gain weight.

One morning, Sharon opened a jug of milk and dropped the seal ring on the floor. Jasper pounced on it and batted it about.

"You'll play with anything." Sharon giggled.

Jasper played with simple toys - string, a stuffed frog with catnip inside, a Kickeroo. And Sharon laughed. After a play session, Sharon lifted her Siamese and kissed him.

"I love you, Jasper. Time for a bath. It's getting late."

She put him down and went into the bathroom. She took off her clothes and stood in front of the mirror. She felt each breast. For three years, she found nothing. Tonight, she discovered a small lump.

When Sharon's MD opened his clinic the next morning, she made an appointment for a half an hour later. After the examination, his assistant made Sharon an appointment for a mammogram and ultrasound, and he sent her for blood tests. A biopsy concluded: cancer.

The lump would be removed followed by chemotherapy. Sharon found the disease early so she chose not to have her breast removed - just a lumpectomy. The Foothills Hospital in Calgary called and scheduled her surgery date. Chemotherapy treatments would begin afterward.

Sharon put her affairs in order. She took a leave of absence from her job as a receptionist at the methanol plant, packed up her belongings, and put the boxes in storage. She gave her landlord notice and took Jasper to his temporary home. She sat in her car and put her hands together.

"Dear God, I am not a religious person by any means, but please help me through this and get me home to Jasper."

And she drove to Calgary.

Chapter Five

Eight days after Jasper arrived, Vera walked by her bed to get her television-watching glasses. The next episode of "Downton Abbey" was coming on. She picked up her glasses, and something grabbed her ankle. She let out a startled screamed and looked down.

Two dark brown and white paws wrapped around her leg. The rest of Jasper hid under the bed.

"What are you doing, you naughty--"

Jasper let her go and raced out from under the bed and sprinted down the hall.

"Naughty. You almost gave me a heart attack. Bad cat. Soon, Jasper. Soon."

Vera sighed. She took her glasses into the living room and sat on the couch. She put her glasses on and turned on the t.v. Her show started several minutes later. She wrapped herself up in the British show and when it ended, she gazed down to her lap.

"When did you get on me? You are some kind of cat, Jasper."

Vera stayed where she sat, and Jasper slept for twenty minutes. He awoke and jumped down. Vera got up and went to her bedroom. She changed into her gardening clothes and headed outside into her backyard. She knelt down by her flowerbed and inspected the tulips and Easter lilies, touching each blossom.

"Easter lilies look so lovely right now."

She smelt the flower with a deep breath. She dug into the soil around the flowers and uprooted two Easter lilies. After slicing off the roots, Vera returned indoors with her pick. Collecting a glass vase from the kitchen cupboard, she filled it with the lilies and some water. She placed the vase on the coffee table and revisited her garden, checking on her young vegetables.

Thirty minutes of pruning, digging and watering slipped by, and she finished for the day.

"Everything looks great."

Vera came back inside and exchanged her dirty clothes for a clean blouse and pants. She retreated to the living room where Jasper stood with paws on the coffee table, sniffing the Easter lilies. He reached up with one paw.

"Get away from those, Jasper. You stink."

She clapped her hands and leaned toward him. Jasper dropped to the floor. He tore out of the living room and down the stairs.

"Darn cat."

She inspected the flowers. No damage.

She rested back into the furniture. With pursed lips, she let out a breath. She picked up the Anne Frank book off the end table and cracked the spine at the bookmark. She read until suppertime.

Jasper stood beside his food dish and meowed and meowed and meowed. Vera stood up and entered the kitchen.

"You hungry?"

And he meowed some more.

"It's a little early to be feeding you."

"Meow."

"Say please."

Jasper kept the noise going and walked back and forth and in circles by his dish. He rubbed her legs. She opened the container of cat food and poured some into his bowl. He ripped into his meal.

"Are you starving, Jasper? You don't look like you're starving?"

Jasper ate, and Vera's stomach growled. She cooked up some Cheemos perogies and Sweetlets peas with one sausage. She ate, but Jasper finished first. He sat and licked his chops beside her. Afterwards, she cleaned up and ate a Dairy Milk chocolate bar for dessert. She settled in to watch a "Law & Order" repeat. Jasper sat beside her then turned his interest to the lilies. He leapt onto the coffee table and sniffed the flowers. Vera shooed him away.

"No."

Jasper jumped down and lay on the carpet.

After the cops and lawyers show, Vera changed the channel to the "Langston Falls News." After some stock market and political news, a story featured a Siamese kitten stuck in a drainage pipe.

"Glad that's not you, Jasper. That kitten could have died."

When nine o'clock rolled around, the old woman and the young Siamese went to bed.

*

In the morning, Vera awoke and visited the bathroom.

Where's Jasper? He usually follows me in here, meowing for food. Did he get into the cat food again. But I put that away - he couldn't've.

She left the loo and checked the kitchen - no Jasper. She stepped downstairs and cleaned out the litter box.

The clumps are bigger this morning - twice as big. He must've drank a lot of water last night.

Her legs ached standing back up and climbing the stairs. She searched for him.

"Jasper? Where are you? Jasper? Something's wrong. Where is he?"

She combed the house - under the bed, behind the couch and t.v. stand. The flowers on the coffee table had only stems left.

"That little--Jasper you ate my lilies. Bad cat."

She searched some more and found him under the china cabinet. He lay curled up. Some vomit pooled beside him and saliva dripped from his chin.

He's sick.

She stood up and called the vet.

"Cypress Hills Veterinarian Clinic. Is this an emergency or can I put you on hold?" a woman said.

"It's an emergency. My granddaughter's cat is sick."

"Tell me what happened."

"He threw up and he's drooling and he won't eat and he won't come out from the cabinet. I think he's sick. I need to bring him in."

"Has he eaten anything unusual?"

"I don't - the Easter lilies!"

"Bring him immediately. As fast as you can."

Vera hung up, rushed to the cat carrier and picked it up. After getting to the cabinet, she bent down in pain and scooped Jasper up. She slid him inside the cat cage and shut the gate. She put her shoes on and hurried to her SUV, carrying the sick feline. She placed him on the front passenger seat and got in. Driving away, she broke every speed law on the way to the vet. The trip took ten minutes.

Vera carried Jasper inside, and the veterinarian assistant ushered them into an examination room. She waited less than a minute for the vet to arrive.

"I'm Dr. Marlen. I understand he's eaten some lilies."

"Yes. Easter lilies I had on the table."

"Easter lilies are poisonous to cats."

"Oh, God. Is he going to be okay?"

"Let's get him on the counter." He opened the gate and drew Jasper out. Dr. Marlen examined him with a stethoscope and ran his hands over the Siamese.

"He appears dehydrated. Lilies can cause kidney failure. We need to give him some activated charcoal and an intravenous for fluids. I'll take him now."

The doctor picked up Jasper and left the room.

"You can wait out here," he said and nodded toward the waiting area.

Dr. Marlen disappeared into the back of the clinic. Vera sat down. She fidgeted and rubbed her shaking hands together. She stared down the corridor where the vet had taken Jasper. Time crawled.

Dr. Marlen reappeared after a slow, long wait. He walked to her, and she stood up. They went into an exam room and shut the door.

"All right, we've got him on an IV to help with the dehydration and some charcoal into his stomach to absorb the poison. I'll be honest. It'll be a struggle to keep him alive. His kidneys may have shut down."

"Oh, you have to help him. Please help him."

"We're doing everything we can. Now, we have to keep giving him fluids and hope for the best. I'd like to keep him over night."

"Yes, keep him as long as you need."

"You can call us in the morning to see how he's doing."

"I will. Please do your best. He's my granddaughter's cat."

"I've got to get back," Dr. Marlen said. "Take care."

The vet turned and vacated the room. Vera approached the receptionist.

"Will he be okay?"

"Dr. Marlen is the best. He'll take good care of him."

Vera forced a smile and left the clinic. She walked to her SUV - every step ached. Once inside the vehicle, she wailed.

"Jasper's going to die. I just know it. Lord, please help him. Hold on, Jasper. Hold on."

Chapter Six

Vera Appleton and James Boxton married July 10, 1961. The next fours years saw two pregnancies - a boy followed by a girl. Gordon - named after Vera's deceased father and Helen - named after James' mother.

Playing outside one day in 1967, Gordon ran across the street, chasing his sister outside their home, and was struck and killed by a speeding 1964 Mustang. A few weeks after Gordon's funeral, the Boxtons adopted a puppy for Helen, who had cried every night for her lost big brother.

The dashhound puppy named Lexi played with Helen for hours almost everyday and sometimes Vera joined in. The little girl and her young dog grew and carried on together. Lexi jumped up on her and wagged her tail each day Helen arrived home from school. Helen fed her table scraps from the dinner table against her mother's orders.

Helen often thought of her big brother with Lexi by her side to hug and hold.

Helen grew up and Lexi grew old. The time came to put Lexi down. Helen refused to let it happen, but Lexi's body broke down. The old dashhound died peacefully at a vet clinic in the Spring of 1981.

At eighteen, Helen graduated high school and attended university to study engineering. She finished her degree four years later and got pregnant two years after graduation. Sharon, her only child, took her first crying breath December 3, 1989.

Helen lived the life of single parenthood, never telling the father of Sharon's existence. Their anonymous sex resulted in Sharon, and Helen demanded nothing from him.

Vera and James celebrated a new addition of their own - a nine month old Boxer named Billy - a tall, gentle loveable pooch. James suffered a massive heart attack and died three days later in hospital. Billy turned one year old the next day.

Vera cried for her husband of 29 years. During their marriage, James worked and Vera took care of the household. Although they had savings, Vera found she needed to work and got employment at the local Wal-Mart as a greeter.

Billy kept her company on those lonely days without James. Vera longed to have a man at home. She met Dan at work, and friendship became romance. He drank, but Vera accepted and ignored it. She had a companion. After the honeymoon phase ended, Dan drank more.

"That dog wrecks the furniture and pisses on the floor. Let's get rid of him. If he goes on the rug again, I swear I will kill him," Dan said.

Billy's tail went between his legs whenever Dan entered the room. The Boxer yipped if Dan made any movement toward him.

After an evening of drinking, Dan laid a beating on Billy with a belt. Vera intervened and Dan struck her too. Dan grabbed at Billy's collar and the dog peed on the carpet.

"I'm gonna make sure you don't piss on my rug again." He dragged Billy outside and threw him in the car. Vera trembled.

"Billy."

Dan drove away and returned thirty minutes later.

"You'll never see him again. You didn't deserve that dog anyway."

Vera did not see Billy again. He had killed the dog she was certain.

Dan refused to let another dog in the house. Vera feared leaving him. She avoided him when he drank. When he died of cirrhosis of the liver, the stress drained out of her head, neck and shoulders. Her muscles relaxed. She breathed a sigh of relief.

"I will not remarry," she told the world. "Better to be alone."

No man, no dog, no one. Until Jasper.

Chapter Seven

Vera stopped crying and gathered herself. She wiped her eyes with a Kleenex and drove away from the animal clinic.

"Why did I bring those damned Easter lilies into the house? It's my fault. All my fault. Jasper's going to die."

She slammed her hand on the steering wheel and swerved across the yellow line. A man in a GMC Jimmy hit the brakes and drove onto the shoulder to avoid her. A close one. Vera pulled back into her lane. Her heart thumped in her throat.

"Oh, God. I'm so awful."

She got home, parked in the garage and made for the flowerbed. She knelt beside the Easter lilies and ripped them out of the soil by the roots. She studied the other flowers and tore those out too.

"I don't deserve flowers."

She piled the plants up beside her. A groan came out of her mouth when she stood up. She gathered the flowers in her arms and strode to the back gate. She opened the latch, stepped through and bumped her arm on a metal fence post.

"Darn fence." She rubbed the wounded spot.

She got to the garbage can and opened the lid, flinging the flowers into the plastic trash bin.

"Noxious weeds."

She slammed the top down. She drew in a deep breath and went inside.

I need to take him off my mind, but I can't. What will Sharon think? She'll be devastated when I tell her. And it's all my fault. She'll never forgive me. I'll never see her or Jasper again.

"Oh, Jasper, please be all right."

Vera made some blueberry tea and loaded it with three sugar cubes. Two more than usual. She sat at the table.

Should I call the vet? It's too soon. This waiting is unbearable.

She drank her tea, rinsed the cup and settled in the living room. She turned on the t.v. Any show would do. "The Price Is Right" came on.

I haven't watched a game show for a while.

After the Showcase Showdown, Vera picked up the television remote control. A bruise the size of a golf ball on the arm she had bumped on the post caught her eye.

"How did I get such a big bruise? It didn't even hurt."

She rubbed the wound. A slight pain. She shrugged and switched the channel to the noon hour news.

Lunchtime, but I don't want to eat. I don't feel like it.

At 4:35pm, she dialed the animal clinic. A veterinarian assistant answered.

"How's Jasper doing?" she asked her.

She put her on hold and Doctor Marlen came on the phone a few minutes later.

"We've been keeping him hydrated, but he hasn't peed. And if he doesn't go means his kidneys have shut down. Which could be fatal. We're watching him, and we should know more in the morning."

"Thank you." Vera hung up.

Poor Jasper. This whole thing is driving me crazy. I'm guilty. This not knowing is killing me. It's going to be a long night.

Vera rubbed her eyes, her lids drifted downward. She yawned.

Better go to bed early.

She didn't eat supper. She turned on the t.v. without watching it. Her head bobbed and her eyes closed and opened. She went into the master bedroom and changed into her blue nightgown.

Blue like Jasper's eyes.

She sat on the bed. She nodded off. She snapped her head up with eyes open. The clock/radio read 8:47pm.

How long did I sleep sitting here?

She stood up and pulled the sheets back. Vera slid between the covers. She shivered and pulled a blanket up to her chin. After turning off the lamp, she drifted away.

*

During the second year of her marriage to Dan, Vera's daughter contracted breast cancer. Helen's sickness was too advanced to treat. They tried and failed. The killer spread to her lymph nodes and lungs. Helen Boxton died at thirty years of age. Sharon lost her mother at five.

Dan refused to allow Sharon to move in with them. Placed into foster care, Sharon joined a strict family with little love. Her foster parents homed several cats and one caught Sharon's eye.

Fuzzy, a medium length coat grey tabby, attached herself to Sharon. The cat would curl up on Sharon's lap as she did homework, watch t.v. or listen to the radio in her bedroom. Fuzzy followed Sharon about the home and cuddled with her as she slept. Sharon kissed and hugged her whenever she wished and Fuzzy stayed still for the kitty loving. When Sharon graduated high school, she moved out of her foster home.

"May I take Fuzzy with me?" she asked.

"She's not your cat," her foster mother said. "So, no."

"You treated me like dirt. The only love I had in this hell home was that cat. And I can't take him?"

"He's not your cat. Now, take your clothes and get out."

Sharon left without saying good-bye to the precious feline. She cried for Fuzzy.

"I will not give up another cat again".

She never returned to the foster home or saw Fuzzy again.

*

Vera awoke at 8:30am.

"Oh no. I've slept twelve hours. I need to call the vet."

She called and spoke to Dr. Marlen.

"Good news, Vera. Jasper peed last night and again this morning. His kidneys seem fine. I examined him again. He's no longer dehydrated and everything tests normal. You can come and get him."

"Delightful news. Delightful. Thank you. Thank you. I'll be there shortly."

Vera got off the phone, raised her arms and shook them.

"Yippee," she said. "I have to pee."

She did and washed. A few pinpoint spots appeared on her hands.

Nothing to worry about because Jasper's better. And that's all that matters.

Chapter Eight

Jasper meowed the following morning, waking Vera up. She sat up and Jasper leapt onto the bed. He stepped up the blanket and bonked his head into hers.

"Oh, Jasper. You're better."

He purred and pushed into her.

"Are you hungry?"

Vera got up and Jasper got down. He ran into the kitchen with Vera following. She undid the child - or rather cat - safety clip from the cupboard with the cat food inside. She measured out a quarter cup of the dry morsels and poured it into his dish. Jasper ate.

"Slow down, kitty. You eat like you're starving...Well, I guess after being sick, you would be quite hungry."

Vera made a piece of toast with raspberry jam and a cup of instant coffee. She sat at the kitchen table and ate. She checked the time - 8:05am. She showered and got ready for cribbage at the Veiner Hall, the local seniors center. The phone rang. Sharon's number appeared in the call display. Vera answered.

"Hello, darling."

"Hi, Grandma. How are you? How's Jasper?"

"We're both fine."

I won't tell her about Jasper eating the Easter lilies. It'll upset her when she doesn't need to worry. She has to get better first.

"Has he been any trouble?"

"No trouble at all."

"Oh, good. Can you keep caring for him a little longer?"

"Yes, dear. I'd be glad to. Is everything okay?"

"The treatments have taken it right out of me. I need more time to recover. I miss my Jasper though."

"How are you doing?"

"I'm exhausted, Grandma. I get tired so easily now. I wish this would just go away. Give Jasper a kiss for me. Thanks, Grandma. I love you."

"I love you too, darling."

They said their good-byes and hung up.

"My poor girl."

Vera's legs ached when she bent down and picked up Jasper. She kissed the top of his head.

This is a first. I've never kissed a cat before. Soft.

"That's from your mommy."

Jasper jumped down and went to his food dish. It was 8:45am.

"Fifteen minutes. I've got to get moving."

Vera rushed into her bedroom and changed her clothes. She returned to the kitchen and got the tray of quartered sandwiches she made for the potluck brunch. She headed out the backdoor and stopped.

"Darn, I forgot my purse."

She stepped in and retrieved her handbag. She went back outside the open door, turned and locked her house shut.

"I'm going make it in time," she said and drove away.

She did not check on Jasper.

Chapter Nine

Vera arrived at the Veiner Hall at two minutes to nine. She put the sandwiches on the potluck table and found her fellow cribbage players. She sat down at their table. They set up the board and dealt the cards.

They started the game and talked - each sharing the events of their week. Mitch informed everyone of his trip to Arizona to visit his doctor-son again. Else spent the week helping other seniors clean their homes. John's one-year-old Scottish terrier tore his slippers apart. And Vera told the Easter lily story.

"He loves his treats," she continued. "I shake the bag and he runs as fast as he can. He'd only eat treats if I let him. He likes to sleep with me. Every time I lie down for a nap, I wake up and he's next to me sleeping. Sometimes he runs around for no reason. He's so funny. He loves to play with milk jug cap rings. I accidentally dropped one on the floor and he batted it around all morning. He's so cute. I love him."

Vera gasped and held her hand to her mouth.

"What's wrong?" Else asked.

"I love a cat. Me? A dog person? I love that always hungry, mischievous, playful, ball of brown, black and white fur, naughty kitty."

The three stared at her.

"I don't want Sharon to take him back when she's better. But he's her cat. I don't want him to go. But he's not my cat."

"I guess you'll have to," said John.

"You could get another cat," Else said.

"There's not another Jasper. I know it."

"Let's play," Mitch said and dealt the next hand.

They played until brunch. Vera's corned beef and mustard sandwiches were devoured first. The thirty-two seniors in attendance finished brunch and visited for another hour or so. Afterwards, Vera left and stopped at the IGA Grocery Store for some milk, chocolate bars and some Temptations cat treats. When she arrived home, she took her groceries inside.

"Jasper."

He did not come.

"Jasper?"

Still no Siamese cat.

Vera retrieved the cat treats and shook the bag.

Nothing.

Is he sick again?

She searched the house - under, upper and in-between. No Jasper.

Oh no, did he get out? He must have. But how? When I came back in to get my purse, I left the door open, but I didn't see him get out. How could I be so stupid?

She raced to the back door and swung it open.

"Jasper. Jasper."

She checked the yard and garden and peered over the neighbors' fences.

"Come on, Jasper. Come on."

"Are you looking for your cat?" Jessica, Vera's neighbor, asked. "I heard you calling so I came out. Is he Siamese?"

"Yes, yes. Have you seen him?"

"After you left this morning, I saw him go across the street."

"Across the street? He could get hit by a car."

Jessica pointed to the open field with tall grass on the other side of road.

"Oh, God. There's coyotes, foxes and rattlesnakes in there. We have to find him. Will you help me?"

"I really don't have the time," Jessica said.

"Oh, please? I need your help. He could get hurt."

Her neighbor nodded, and they headed to the field.

"He'll be hard to find in those weeds, but we'll try."

"Thank you so much."

They combed through the grass, looking with strained necks.

"Jasper," they called.

After an hour, Jessica said, "I don't think he's here. I have to go home. The kids will be home from school soon. Sorry, Vera. Lots of times cats come back on their own. You just have to wait."

"I guess you're right. I don't think he's here either."

Vera's shoulders slumped. They walked back to their homes. Vera opened the gate to her backyard and went around the house. Jasper sat on the doormat.

"Jasper! I found him," Vera yelled.

Her heart rate accelerated and she ran to him. She picked him up and hugged and kissed him, missing what lay on the mat beside him.

"Don't ever do that to me again."

She kissed him some more. A dead mouse rested below.

"You brought me a gift, Jasper? How gross."

Chapter Ten

"Hi, Grandma," Sharon said, her voice chipper.

"Hi, honey. How are you?"

"I'm feeling much better now. My cancer is in remission. I'm on my way back to town. I can't wait to see you and my kitty."

"I knew this day would come," Vera said after a long pause. *But I'm not ready for it.*

"Grandma? Everything good? Can I come and pick him up tomorrow?"

"Yes, dear." Her voice cracked.

"Grandma, are you alright?"

"I'm fine, dear. I'll see you tomorrow."

Vera hung up without saying "good-bye."

She held back tears. Jasper slept on the recliner and she went to him. She picked him up. He meowed. She held him and kissed his whiskers.

"Tomorrow is too soon."

*

In the morning, Vera fed Jasper. After cleaning out his litter box, she carried it upstairs.

I won't miss this box. That's for sure. Even though, he's worth it.

Vera didn't eat breakfast even though her stomach told her to. She took the cat carrier out of the closet and placed it by the front door. She turned on CHAT Radio for some country music. An Alabama song played. Vera sat and listened. Jasper joined her and stretched across her lap.

"I'm going to miss you, my Siameser."

She stroked his back and he purred.

*

A little after lunch, Sharon knocked. Vera put Jasper aside and answered the door. Sharon entered and hugged her grandmother. Vera smiled with her lips pressed together.

"You know, he's been a real good cat."

"Thank you for taking care of him. Where is my Jasper?"

"Do you want to come in and visit?"

"Can we do that another day? I've got lots to do today."

"Okay, Sharon. Jasper's on the couch."

Sharon took Jasper off the couch and smothered him with kisses.

"I missed you so much, my furry face."

Sharon brought him the carrier and bent down to push him in.

"Can I say 'good-bye' to him?" Vera said.

"Of course, Grandma."

Sharon placed Jasper into Vera's outstretched arms. Vera held him, petting and kissing the Siamese. Tears pooled in her eyes.

"I'm gonna miss you, Jasper."

Her chin trembled when she handed him back to Sharon. She took him and tears rolled down Vera's face.

"You really love him, don't you?"

Vera nodded and wiped her tears away with a tissue from her pocket.

"I'll be all right."

"Do you want to keep him?" Sharon asked.

"What? Yes! No. I can't."

"Why not?"

"He's yours."

"Now...he's yours."

"I can't take him away from you."

"You're not. I'm giving him to you. Don't you want him?" Vera smiled.

"Yes."

"Is it all right if I come and visit him though?"

"Yes. Anytime."

Vera hugged her granddaughter with Jasper between them. After a while, Sharon released Vera and gave the kitty good-bye loves. She left holding back her own tears. Vera waved to her as she drove away. Vera smiled the entire day and night and fell asleep still grinning.

Chapter Eleven

A few weeks past and Vera and Jasper played and cuddled. Sharon stopped in every week or so loving Jasper and visiting with Vera.

*

One Saturday afternoon, Sharon knocked on Vera's door several times before the elderly woman answered. Vera cracked the door open.

"Grandma, what's wrong?"

Sharon stepped in and Vera backed away from her.

"Just the flu. You better not get too close. Can you come back another day?"

"You're bleeding. Did Jasper scratch your hand?"

"No, I hit it on the door knob."

"And what happened to your face?"

"I don't know. I woke up with it. I must have hit the headboard in my sleep."

"Grandma, that's a big bruise. You've lost weight. Have you been eating?"

"I'm not hungry."

Sharon kissed her forehead.

"You have a fever. I'm taking you in. Who's your doctor?"

"Doctor Richards. But he's not open today. I'm so tired."

"I'm taking you to emergency. Something's wrong. Let's get your shoes on."

"And a sweater. I'm cold."

Sharon put her shoes on for her and the sweater too. She got her to the car and drove her to the hospital.

*

At admitting, Sharon and Vera explained her symptoms and were directed to the waiting room. Four minutes later, a nurse entered with a wheelchair and took Vera to Emergency Room Two. She took her temperature and checked her pulse.

"You need to put this gown on," the nurse said and left.

"I'll help you," Sharon said.

Soon, Vera's gown hung on her thin frame. A man dressed in a lab coat pulled the curtain aside and entered the room.

"I'm Doctor Jacobs. I understand you've been having some flu-like symptoms."

"Yes. She's bruising and bleeding easily too."

Jacobs picked up Vera's hand and asked, "How long have you had these pinpoint spots?"

"Oh, for a while."

He examined her some more.

"How long have you felt sick with the flu?"

"On and off for a while."

"How long? Days? Weeks? Months?"

"More than a few weeks."

"Your lymph nodes are swollen. You're pale. Do you know where you got these bruises from?"

"No."

"Why didn't you say something before?" Sharon asked.

"I'm an old woman. I get tired."

"Have you had any nosebleeds or unusual bleeding?"

"Yes, nosebleeds."

"I'm ordering some tests. Someone from the lab will be here shortly," the doctor said.

Jacobs exited the room.

Sharon sighed.

She should've seen her doctor before. But if I say something, it will upset her, Sharon thought.

The curtain opened and a woman entered with a tray on a cart.

"I'm Leslie. I'm from the lab and I need to take some blood."

Leslie drained some blood from Vera's right arm. She placed a cotton ball surrounded by tape on the injection hole in Vera's arm. Leslie left. And they waited.

*

Sharon sat at the foot of the bed when Doctor Jacobs re-entered the room after a long wait - his face dour.

"Mrs. Boxton, you have leukemia. A rather aggressive form of the disease called acute myeloid leukemia. We need to do more blood tests to see how far the cancer has gone. You shouldn't have waited so long to see a doctor. Someone will take you upstairs to a room. We'll get the blood test called a CBC for complete blood count done as soon as possible."

Sharon's heart caved in and knocked the wind out of her. She gasped.

"Oh, Grandma."

Vera stayed silent. The blood drained out of her face.

*

After more tests, Vera rested in the hospital's west wing with Sharon by her side. Dr. Jacobs came in with the test results.

"Mrs. Boxton, I have bad news. The cancer has taken a toll on you. Your white blood cells are extremely elevated and your red blood cells and platelets are very low. There is nothing we can do. The leukemia is so pervasive that any treatments would be ineffective. It is terminal. At best, you have two maybe three weeks until you pass."

"No, not possible," Vera said.

"I'm afraid so. You will need to get your affairs in order. We will make a call to General County Hospice, and you'll be transferred there when a bed comes available."

Sharon held her grandmother and they wept. The doctor excused himself. Vera stopped crying and held Sharon's face.

"I knew this day would come, eventually. I am old, Sharon, honey. Please take Jasper back and care of him for me. He's yours again."

"I will, Grandma." Sharon wiped her tears.

"And could you call my attorney? His name is Thorston Young and tell him to come and see me right away."

"Yes, I will."

"I need some rest, honey. Please get Jasper and call Mr. Young. I need to be alone right now."

"All right."

She kissed Vera on the cheek. She stepped outside the room and gathered herself.

"Dear Lord, I'm on my way. Please forgive me for the sins I have committed during my life. And, more importantly, please watch over Sharon and Jasper. They only have each other now."

Chapter Twelve

The next morning, Vera's lawyer attended to her in her room.

"In my will, I want everything to got to my granddaughter so she can take care of herself and Jasper. Also..."

Vera pushed a breath of air through her lips.

"I want a 'do not resuscitate' order in place when I'm dying."

Young wrote it all down on his laptop and printed the forms. Vera signed the documents and they parted.

*

That afternoon, a nurse came into Vera's room.

"There is an opening at the hospice. You'll be transferred there in the morning."

"Thank you. I don't want to be burden on the hospital. Other people need this bed."

Her bruising and bleeding worsened. A fever made her shiver. She refused food so they put her on intravenous fluids. Vera slept on and off throughout the day. Sharon returned that evening.

"Grandma, how are you doing?"

"As good as I can be. A bed opened up and they're moving me in the morning. Someone died."

"Oh, Grandma."

"How's Jasper? I wish I could see him. But they won't let cats up here. Maybe in the hospice. I really miss him. He's such a kitty."

"He's doing fine. I'll see what I can do when you go to the hospice."

Sharon stayed and talked with her until Vera fell asleep.

*

Morning came and two men dressed in scrubs arrived and moved Vera to a gurney. They wheeled her to the paramedics, waiting at the ambulance. The paramedics, a man and a woman, greeted Vera and lifted her in the EMS transport. The woman rode in the back with Vera with the other paramedic driving to the hospice.

Smiling staff welcomed Vera to the hospice, and soon she lay in a firm bed in a private room. She rested. A nurse entered and asked her some questions.

"I'm sinking and I want to see Jasper."

"Who's Jasper?" the nurse asked.

"He's my cat."

"I'm sorry, Mrs. Boxton, we don't allow pets in here. We have sick people here who could get an infection or be disturbed by the presence of a cat," the nurse said and left.

"I want my baby," Vera said. Her chin quivered.

*

After work, Sharon visited Grandma in the hospice. Vera appeared pasty and pale with small red dots on her arms. And more bruising too. Sharon sat in the chair beside the bed. Vera opened her eyes.

She looks so sad, Sharon thought.

"Sharon?"

"I'm here, Grandma. How are you feeling?"

"I'm fine, I guess. A little tired. It's so good to see you. How's Jasper?"

"He's just fine. Meows a lot. I think he misses you. I picked him up yesterday. He's adjusting to my new apartment. I'm not allowed pets there, but I snuck him in. I'm going to find a new place that allows cats."

"I want to see Jasper, but they won't let me."

"Who won't let you?"

"The staff here."

Vera pulled up the blanket and shook.

"Grandma, you let me worry about that."

Sharon stood up and walked out to the nurse's station and stared the woman behind the counter in the eye.

"My grandmother wants to see Jasper. Do you allow cats in here?"

"No, we don't."

"Why not?"

"They could cause an infection or allergic reaction in our patients. Also, some of our residents may be scared of or hate cats. We try to keep everyone as comfortable as possible."

"My grandma is not comfortable because she cannot see him."

"I'm sorry, we have to look at our patients as a whole. Some of our people suffer from delusions as they get closer to passing. A cat can exacerbate the problem. These patients need rest, peace and comfort, and a cat can disturb them."

"But if her kitty is in her room with the door closed, there's no chance he'll affect anyone else."

"Nope, sorry."

"Listen, my grandmother is almost gone. Jasper and I are all she has. Please let me bring him to see her. He will make her happy in her final days. She's begging to see him."

A doctor walked up to them and listened. The nurse shook her head "no."

"What's going on?"

"They won't let me bring my grandmother's cat in so she can see him one last time," Sharon said.

"Those are the rules here. We cannot allow any pets in here," the doctor said.

"But it would mean so much to a dying old lady."

"No."

169

Sharon made a fist and walked back to Vera's room. She sat with the ailing woman until they both grew weary. Vera slept and Sharon went home.

How can I get Jasper in to see her? I'm not giving up. But what can I do?

Chapter Thirteen

Over the next few days, Vera's condition worsened. The nurses inserted a catheter into her bladder. Her weakness prevented her from using the toilet. She lay motionless in her bed most of the day. They injected her IV with morphine for the pain. Sharon visited often.

*

Sharon's phone rang on a Saturday morning. She answered it.

"Vera had a rough night last night," the nurse said. "The doctor doesn't think she'll last the day."

Sharon hung up, dressed and put Jasper in his carrier.

"I'm doing this whether they like it or not."

She took Jasper and headed to the hospice.

*

Sharon brought Jasper into the building. The receptionist stopped her at the entrance.

"You can't bring that cat in here."

"It's my grandmother's last day on earth so I'm bringing him in."

"You can't bring it in here."

"Just watch me."

Sharon pushed past the receptionist and strode down the corridor toward Vera's room.

"Hey, come back here. I'm calling security."

Sharon made it to Vera's room and took Jasper inside.

She looks dead. Did I get here in time?

A doctor stood by her heart monitor, focused on it. Jasper meowed.

"Grandma, I have Jasper."

The doctor turned and Vera opened her eyes.

"Jasper?"

"I have him."

Sharon set the carrier on the chair and opened the gate. She took him out. Vera raised her hand and touched him. Sharon put Jasper on the bed beside Vera. Jasper sniffed at her and settled in beside her. Vera lifted her head and smiled.

"Thank you, honey."

Vera lay her hand on the soft Siamese. Jasper curled beside her, pushed his head into her hand and purred.

"Her heart rate is up a little," the doctor said.

Sharon followed the doctor's eyes to the monitor and back to Vera and Jasper. Vera smiled.

A security guard opened the door and came in with the receptionist behind him.

"You have to get that cat out of here," she said.

"Ma'am, you have to leave," the security guard said.

"Jasper, no," Vera said.

Her smile faded and her heart rate spiked.

"It's all right," the doctor said. "The cat can stay."

"But it is not allowed," the receptionist said.

"You are upsetting my patient. Please leave the room."

The woman shook her head and exited the room with the security guard behind her.

"You can stay here with Jasper as long as you like. He has a good effect on her. Maybe we should rethink our pet policy."

Sharon smiled and Vera's heart rate calmed. The doctor stepped out of the room.

Jasper stayed by Vera's side the rest of the day and into the night. Nurses and the doctor went in and out through the day and night, checking on the old woman and her cat.

"She's lasted longer than we thought," the doctor said to Sharon.

*

In the morning, Vera died with Jasper curled beside her and a smile on her face.

When they came to take Vera's body away, Sharon gathered up Jasper and tucked him into the carrier. She sat and mourned. Jasper did not meow.

"She's gone, Jasper."

*

Vera Boxton's funeral service occurred three days later. Sharon returned to work the next day. She sat at her desk and thought.

How she loved Jasper...and maybe me too.

Chapter Fourteen

Sharon sat in the lunchroom and took out her iPhone. A voicemail waited. She listened to it. Mr. Young called to make an appointment for the reading of the will. Sharon returned his call and booked a time in two days.

That day at 9:30am with only Sharon in attendance, the lawyer read the will.

"She left everything to you."

After the final arrangements, Sharon and Jasper moved into Vera's old house - free and clear. Vera also willed Sharon $260,595.00 she had saved in a retirement account.

"That's a whole lot of cat food for you, Jasper. Best cat ever," Sharon said, hugging and kissing her Siamese.

"Thank you, Grandma."

Thank You

Thank you for buying and reading this book and for trusting me to entertain you. I hope you'll consider writing a blurb about "The Christmas Cat Tails" online in the book listing's review section at any online retailer. It would be a huge honor if you did. And very much appreciated!

Best wishes always,

Peter

Also By This Author

How To Litter Train Your Cat:
Why Your Kitty Is Going Outside The Box & How To
Stop It

The Wonder of Cats:
With Hundreds of Fascinating Feline Facts Waiting
Inside To Be Discovered

How Do Cats Do That?
Discover How Cats Do The Amazing Things They Do

All Available Online
And at Your Local Bookstore

Follow Peter Scottsdale
(@PScottsdale)
on Facebook

About the Author

A cat lover from an early age, Peter Scottsdale wrote his first cat tale, "The Cat and the Dog," in a grade three creative writing exercise – the story of a cat and a dog lost in the woods, and the police shooting the dog for some reason. Peter drew inspiration for the story from Disney's *The Incredible Journey*.

Inspired by such books as Hardy Boys Mysteries, Marvel Comics and *Mythology* by Edith Hamilton, Scottsdale wrote several published short stories with his grade nine English teacher.

Then life happened. Scottsdale stopped writing, only scribbling bits of story every so often. A family came along which turned into single parenthood. He raised his kids and wrote here-and-there.

Throughout his life, cats have been a welcome and influencing presence. From Tia (a Siamese) to Booties (a Tabby with White) to Rusty (an orange boy with little ears) to Sam the Siamese, Peter has loved all his felines (and still does). He's loved all his cats so much so he started to write about them. They have inspired and delighted him to create cat stories and to find feline facts for his books.

Cat lover turned author, Peter Scottsdale published his first book, *365 Fascinating Facts You Didn't Know About Your Cat*, in 2012. He followed that with "The Christmas Cat" and more cat books both in print and as ebooks – all available online.

An English Major, Scottsdale graduated from Medicine Hat College with an Associate of Arts Diploma in 1995. He continues to research our furry felines and write cat fiction and non-fiction and hopes fellow kitty-cat people will enjoy his work.

Currently, he resides in Medicine Hat, AB with his three cats: Tanzy (the feisty feline), Alley (the mischief maker) and Tigger (the gentle giant).

Made in the USA
Lexington, KY
19 September 2018